Faith, Hope, and
Chicken Feathers

Faith, Hope, and Chicken Feathers

ANDREA WYMAN

Holiday House/New York

Library of Congress Cataloging-in-Publication Data
Wyman, Andrea.
Faith, hope, and chicken feathers / Andrea Wyman.
p.   cm.
Summary: Sophie, YL, and Harper, new students in Mrs. TenBroeck's
sixth grade class, give each other support as they struggle to
survive both in and out of school.
ISBN 0-8234-1117-6
[1. Schools—Fiction. 2. Identity—Fiction.] I. Title.
PZ7.W9788St   1994   93-26293   CIP   AC
[Fic]—dc20

A special note of thanks goes to the following individuals for their assistance: Lynne and Henry Muller; Jane Foust; Irene Jacobs and the students in her fifth-grade class at Margaret Bell Miller Middle School; Ted Sohier; Timothy Hawfield; Farley Mowat; Sue Webb; David Yue; Cristine Shaw; Paul H. Jensen; and G.G.

In 1991, I received the Ezra Jack Keats Award, sponsored by the Kerlan Collection, a children's literature research collection at the University of Minnesota. I would like to thank the Ezra Jack Keats Foundation, Inc., and the members of the Kerlan Collection staff for their support in the research and writing of this book.

In the parts of this book in which the fictional story *Children of the Northern Lights* is read, the specific wording relating to native cultures reflects the following: I used the term Inuit when referring to native Arctic people; the term Netsilik, or netsilingimiut, applies to one particular grouping of the Inuit. They are known as seal hunters, or "listeners at the breathing places in the ice." The Netsilik are a northernmost, native Arctic people whose remarkable skills help them survive even the harshest winter months.

A.W.

May 1993

*Always for Rick, Susan, and Drew,
with recognition to a very special
sixth-grade teacher, Carrie E. Shuck,
and the everlasting memories of two friends,
Lee Aldridge Dillon, 1948–1961, and
Shiue-chien Chu, 1931–1990*

Contents

x CONTENTS

Faith, Hope, and
Chicken Feathers

Prologue

On a Tuesday afternoon in early March, eighteen of the twenty students in Claire TenBroeck's sixth-grade class bolted through the door before the 3:10 bell finished buzzing. At precisely 3:10 P.M. and five seconds, only three people were left in Room 17.

"Sophie, YL," Mrs. TenBroeck called out, her voice sounding strained, "we need to take care of this." She waved a pink phone message in the air. The two students slipped out of their seats and walked slowly to the teacher's desk. The honey-colored wooden floorboards creaked and groaned with each step.

Teacher and students stared at the pink paper as if it might do something, as if it might come alive at any minute, or speak to them, or bite their hands.

"Here," Mrs. TenBroeck said, shoving a brown-paper shopping bag at Sophie, "this ought to hold everything."

"But . . ." Sophie began.

"When you're done, take everything down to the office. Harper's mother will come by to pick up the bag.

I have to see Mr. Workel, he wants to speak to me."
Mrs. TenBroeck's voice broke, and she looked away.
Her face was flushed. Her hands trembled. She headed
toward the door. Her broad shoulders swung from side
to side as she left the room.

Sophie batted open the top of the shopping bag. She
and YL stepped into the old-fashioned cloakroom, tip-
toeing around the litter of boots, gloves, and scarves on
the floor.

Shoved into a forlorn corner, buried beneath a
mound of yellowed posterboard and oaktag, Harper's
desk was barely visible. Rumpled silhouettes from the
February bulletin boards of George Washington and a
valentine cupid lay on top of her desk. It had been
scooted into the cloakroom the day after she'd disappeared. Sophie and YL carefully began to pack the
desk's meager contents into the crinkly brown bag.

One chewed-up, pink pearl eraser. Little slips of paper with smeary thumbprints. An igloo made from rectangular sugar cubes. Two unopened pieces of Bazooka
bubble gum from Harper's stash of valentine candy. A
plastic container of red glitter. An ink pad and a red-
and-yellow booklet titled, Palm and Fingerprint Reading Made Easy. A list of all the swear words Harper
and YL and Sophie knew, written during a boring social studies lesson on temperate zones.

The nearly empty desk contained only a few more
items. A handful of smooth gray rocks, the size of birds'
eggs. A slip of paper with a Tacoma phone number. A
cat's flea collar in a sandwich bag. An admission ticket
to the National Museum of American History.

The contents of the bag jiggled and rattled as YL carried it back into the classroom. Sophie stood behind Mrs. TenBroeck's desk. Room 17, with all its empty desks, seemed even emptier than usual now that Harper was gone.

"Nope," Sophie said aloud. She slapped the top of Mrs. TenBroeck's desk so hard that her palm stung.

"This is not the way it's supposed to be," YL said. His voice was loud. The words ricocheted off the back walls, catching Sophie by surprise. And that was when she knew what they would do. What they must do.

The front of Harper's desk screeched and dug into the floor as Sophie and YL used it to snowplow boots, gloves, and stray scarves out of the cloakroom. The two students shoved and pushed Harper's desk to its original place in the classroom.

"Now, the room is more like it ought to be," YL said. "This is the way we started out."

As Sophie and YL moved toward the door to go to the principal's office and tell Mrs. TenBroeck the job was completed, they hesitated. Instead, Sophie stepped up to the front chalkboard and found a piece of chalk hidden under two erasers in the dusty tray. YL watched. She had something to say about Harper, something different from the rumors Melody Briscoe tried to circulate: Harper had been kidnapped. Harper had a dreaded disease. Harper was dead.

Sophie thought for a minute about what was in her heart and had weighed so heavily on her mind the last few days. She picked up a nub of chalk. Then, in the boldest and thickest and yellowest letters she could man-

*age, she printed her message across the middle of the
chalkboard. YL read her words aloud.*

HARPER LEE STRITCH iS ALiVE AND WELL AND LiViNG ON THE PLANET SATURN!

"That's more like it," Sophie stated, "don't you
think?"

"Right," YL added in agreement.

They stood by the door for a second before YL switched
off the light. Memories of that first day at Whispering
Springs Elementary flooded their minds.

How could they forget the cold, crisp day in January
on a Monday morning when the three of them, YL,
Sophie, and Harper, had stood at the entrance to Room
17? The minute the door had opened, eighteen pairs of
eyes stared at the three new kids.

YL, Sophie, and Harper stood stiff and wooden, nervous and scared in their own separate ways. Three sets
of clammy cold hands. Three churning stomachs. All
the spit having disappeared from their dry mouths. Each
new student, Sophie first, then Harper, followed by YL,
tried to swallow, but it seemed impossible. There was
no room because their pounding hearts had suddenly
jumped into their throats. . . .

CHAPTER ONE

Ladies
and Jelly Beans

"**S**urprise!" Mr. Workel said, sticking his head inside the door of Room 17 the first day of school after Christmas vacation. "Three new kids for your room," the principal announced, reading from the canary-yellow slips of paper in his hand.

"Mizz Harper Lee Stritch from Kenosha, Wisconsin," he said, sounding like a host on a TV game show. He patted her head like she was two years old. "Mister YL Truax here is from . . ." Mr. Workel checked one of the slips of paper. "His father said they just moved from Cheyenne, Wyoming." Mrs. TenBroeck stopped what she was doing at the chalkboard and walked over to the door.

"Is your father with the army?" Mrs. TenBroeck asked, eyeing YL. He stared at the very pointy toes of her high-heeled shoes.

"No, ma'am, he's a disc jockey."

"A disc jockey? Do you mean a disc jockey, as in on-the-radio disc jockey?"

"Yes, ma'am. He works for WMTN."

"Well, I'll be a monkey's uncle. . . ."

Mr. Workel cleared his throat and looked at his watch. Mrs. TenBroeck got the message and stopped her questioning.

"And this is Miss Sophia Maria Spagnolo who's moved to Whispering Springs from Magnolia, Delaware." Mr. Workel pulled one of Sophie's fluffy brown curls. He handed Mrs. TenBroeck the slips of paper. "Sophie's parents are the ones who bought the old Crescent Moon Motel on Route Forty," he added.

"No kidding," Mrs. TenBroeck replied, her eyebrows furrowing. "The *old* Crescent Moon Motel," she muttered.

"Welcome to West Virginia, kids," Mr. Workel said. "I hope I won't see a single one of you down in my office," he finished, pointing his index finger at YL, Sophie, and Harper.

"Why don't you three take the desks in the back of the room for right now?" Mrs. TenBroeck said, pointing to them.

"Citizens! Citizens of Room Seventeen," she commanded, turning to the entire class, "we have new students today." She slipped on a pair of bifocals. The gold charms on her charm bracelets rattled and clanked as she picked up a piece of chalk and began to write on the board. She adjusted her glasses while she read from the slips of paper. She wrote in large sloping letters: *YL Truax, Sophia Maria Spagnolo,* and *Harper Lee Stritch.*

"Let's give our new students a big welcome," she reminded. "Remember our song?" The class audibly groaned, but Mrs. TenBroeck continued her toothy smile. She walked to the center of the room and began waving her arms, the charms jingling. "Make new friends? Remember? Our welcoming song. You remember, don't you?" she admonished, looking at the students. She stepped to the front of the room. "Hmmmmm," she sang, providing the beginning pitch and making sweeping motions in the air as she conducted the class through the song.

"Make new friends, but ke-ep th-e oh-old," the wobbly, thin voices in the first two rows sang. Mrs. TenBroeck's voice chirped above them all. She pointed to the next two rows and the last two, until the whole class was singing rounds.

"One is silver, and the o-ther's gold," the first singers finished. Mrs. TenBroeck continued pointing and conducting until the final two rows of students completed, "and the o-ther's gold." Harper, YL, and Sophie sat in their seats, speechless.

"That was lovely. Simply splendid," Mrs. TenBroeck complimented the class. "Bravo!" she applauded, her claps the only ones in the room. "Now, we'll get back to business. Citizens," she ordered, turning around and walking toward her desk, "take out your social studies books. We have barely enough time before lunch to learn everything you ever wanted to know about the equator." She licked her index finger and flipped through the pages. "Page forty-five, if you will, please, ladies and jelly beans." She looked to the back of the room, noticing the three new students still frozen in place. "Move 'em out, doggies. Hustle, hustle. Get rolling back there. That means you new people, too. There ought to be social studies books in those desks, or my name isn't Claire TenBroeck."

Sophie lifted the lid of the desk and held it with her head. She scooted the slippery books to one side, checking the spines for the words SOCIAL STUDIES. She turned her head and caught the attention of the boy next to her.

"When's lunch?" she asked.

"In two more hours," he whispered.

"Oh," she sighed.

"Melody Briscoe?" Mrs. TenBroeck called out.

"Yes?"

The teacher put on her glasses and ran a red, nail-polished index finger down a long list of printed names on the bulletin board beside her desk. "Melody, it appears from my list here that you're the Welcome Hostess for the month."

Melody Briscoe groaned aloud.

"That means you'll give YL, Sophia, and Harper a tour of the school during the lunch hour. Remember to show them the bookstore and the nurse's office. Got that?"

"Yes, Mrs. TenBroeck," Melody muttered, glaring at Sophie.

*   *   *

"Call me Melo," Melody Briscoe told the three students sitting across from her at the lunch table. Sophie, Harper, and YL looked up from their lunch trays. "So where's Magnolia, Delaware?" Melody quizzed, in between mouthfuls of grilled-cheese sandwich. Sophie's cheek bulged with a big bite of meat loaf. She didn't answer. Melody turned to YL.

"We don't have that many black kids at this school. Were you the only black kid in your school in Cheyenne?"

"Nope," YL answered. He stared at her, amazed that she would ask such a question.

"What a bunch of ko-inky-dinks you are," she said, eyeing the three of them. "You've all started Whispering Springs Elementary School on the same day," she sputtered in between gulps of chocolate milk.

"What's a ko-inky-dink?" Sophie asked.

"Where have you been?" Melody replied. "Were you born in a barn or something? A koinkydink is a coincidence. Can you believe it, Old Tennie's stuck me with a bunch of fruitcakes," Melody exclaimed, shaking her head. "So tell me, YL, do they have a lot of cowboys out in Wyoming?" she asked.

"On ranches," he answered, looking at Melody suspiciously.

"Have you met Carnell yet?"

"Nope. Who's Carnell?"

"Carnell Witherspoon. He's the only other black kid in sixth grade. I'm sure you'll want to be best friends with him."

YL pulled at the collar of his T-shirt.

"And you?" she asked, turning her attention to Harper, "where did they say you were from?"

"Mars," Harper replied, "as in the planet."

YL laughed, and little flecks of mashed potatoes sprayed out of his mouth.

"That's gross," Melody said. "Just my luck," she added scornfully, "Old Tennie's stuck me with the koinkydinks." She stood up, lunch tray in hand. Sophie looked up. Only half the food on her plastic lunch plate was eaten. She liked the meat loaf and mashed potatoes. Harper stopped scooting the peas around the plastic tray with her fork.

"If you want to see the nurse's office and the hole-in-the-wall they call the bookstore, you'd better move it," Melody said, walking toward the dirty-dish conveyor.

YL shook his head.

"What's the matter with you?" Harper asked.

"I wish somebody would tell me," YL said, "why it is that people always think that just because one black person happens to know another black person, they're going to be best friends. There's no law somewhere which says that because two people are black, they're going to like each other."

YL shoveled meat loaf and potatoes into his mouth.

"Yolanda," Harper said suddenly.

"What?" Sophie replied.

"Yolanda."

"Yolanda who?" Sophie asked.

"No, not you, him," Harper offered, pointing to

YL. "I bet your name's Yolanda. Like Yoo, come on over here, Landa. That's what the YL stands for. Yoo Landa."

YL jammed the last piece of meat loaf into his mouth.

"Nope," he answered, looking like a squirrel with a nut in his cheek. He placed his fork on the tray and stood up. "Don't be dumb. Yolanda's a girl's name," he muttered. "Guess all you want. I'm not going to tell you what the YL stands for. All the wild horses in the state of Wyoming couldn't drag it out of me."

"Give me a little time," Harper replied, standing up. "I'll figure it out."

"Where *are* you from?" Sophie asked.

"Saturn," Harper said. "I should've said Saturn. It's a much more exciting planet than Mars."

"Saturn has seventeen moons," YL explained.

"We only have one," Sophie added.

"No duh," Harper answered.

"Are you into stars?" YL asked, hoping to cover up Harper's comment.

"It's not stars, it's more like astronomy. Astrology. Anything like that. I'm a card-carrying member of the Astrologers of the Galaxy."

"Sounds to me like something you get off the back of a cereal box," YL said.

"Shows what you know," Harper stated.

"She called us koinkydinks," Sophie offered, changing the subject. "All I did was ask what the word meant."

"Well, I feel honored," YL explained. "I've lived in

three different cities in the last three years, and I've never been called a koinkydink before. I've been called a geek, a nerd, a dingwat, a dipbrain, but never a koinkydink."

The three koinkydinks rounded a corner and saw Melody with her arms crossed, standing by the door to the nurse's office.

"This is my fifth city in the last six years," Harper explained.

"This is my first move," Sophie said softly. "But I still think Melody was rude to call us koinkydinks. She doesn't even know us yet."

"Well, it's my guess that what we're seeing is probably Melody Briscoe at her best," Harper replied. "Actually, there's nothing wrong with being koinkydinks. We're all probably starting school at Whispering Springs on the same day due to some amazing astrological convergence that old Melo wouldn't have the brainpower to understand." Sophie laughed. "So don't let it bother you," Harper told Sophie, even giving her a light tap on the shoulder. "Look at it this way, Melody could've called us the Three Stooges, and then we'd have to figure out which one of us was Moe and Curly and Larry."

Mrs. Dildine, the nurse, came out of the office with two folders in her hand.

"Who do we have here? Mr. YL Truax, I presume?"

"Yes, ma'am."

"And which one of you is Miss Spagnolo?"

Sophie raised her hand.

"Then I need records from you, dear," the nurse said, turning to Harper. "Technically, you're not even supposed to be in school without your health records. I certainly shouldn't allow you to be here without your immunization records. But," she said, using a Dracula-like voice, "come into my castle."

Melody stood outside the doorway while the three koinkydinks peeked into the small office. Two beds and a desk took up the entire space. The room smelled of alcohol and fresh bars of soap. A door to a small bathroom was ajar.

"She keeps the barf bowls under the bed," Melody added from the hallway.

"That's right," Mrs. Dildine explained, "but I don't see many kids who are that sick. Besides, I double as the gym teacher. I get the minor stuff. I'm the first one to see floor burns, clunked heads, skinned knees, and fat lips," she said, showing them a bottle of pinkish Merthiolate. "But, boy, do I hate dodgeball season. There's nothing worse, in my book, than a jammed thumb." Mrs. Dildine opened a small, whirring refrigerator. "Ice!" she said, letting the door slam. "Always have plenty of ice. That's my motto."

CHAPTER TWO

Sophie, Harper, and YL:
The Koinkydinks

The clock radio beside YL's bed clicked on.

"*Good morning, Morgantowners, that was the Everly Brothers, so wake up, little Susie and wake up little Sandy. It's a good morning, too, an eye-popping Wednesday morning in January, nineteen hundred and eighty-two. The time is exactly six forty-five in the* A.M. *The temperature, a brisk twenty-two degrees, but moving up to the high thirties later in the day, according to the forecast.*" YL heard his father say all this as the digital readout on the clock flipped to 6:46 A.M. YL listened more carefully than usual, wondering if his father had found the sound-effects tape that had been his trademark at the old radio station in Cheyenne. "*You're listening to WMTN, 91.6 on your dial, Morgantown's station for the best in Rock* [chains rattled] *and* [a door creaked open] *Roll* [a fog horn blasted]." YL smiled. His father must've found the sound-effects tape. "*So Rise* [tires screeched] *aaaand* [a cow mooooed] *Shine* [a fire bell clanged]. *Up and at 'em. Let's get those big brown eyes blinking. Those shower pipes humming, Morgantowners."*

Every morning, except Sunday, YL's father was at the radio station by 4:40 A.M. and on the air by five. Having a DJ for a dad made YL different from any of the other kids he knew. Ever since third grade, when his father switched from working nights to working days, YL had gotten used to an independent morning routine. At least with a day shift, YL and his dad stood a chance of seeing each other by early afternoon. That is, if his father didn't have a commercial to tape or an after-school sock hop to host or a shopping mall appearance to make. On this Wednesday morning, YL Truax dug deeper under the covers.

"Move those lazy bones out of bed. You can't fool me. I know you're only burrowing deeper under the covers. I'll read the school lunch menus. That ought to get everyone up and rolling, what do you say? Lunch today is taco burgers with green beans and a side of applesauce. Tomorrow, it's macaroni and cheese. . . ."

YL stared at the radio. How does Dad always know when I don't get up? he asked himself.

"Keep your hand off that snooze alarm, rock-and-roll lovers. It's six forty-seven. Come on now. Here's Bill Haley and the Comets; let him hustle your bustle and shake and rattle and roll you right out of bed."

Music rumbled from YL's radio. He tossed the covers aside and dangled his legs over the edge of the bed. His father had spoken. He knew that while his father might sound like he was talking to every Morgantown listener tuned to 91.6 within a 150-mile radius, he truly intended his morning radio message for one particular sixth grader, namely YL. YL recognized his father's hidden cues. Wake up! Get out of bed! Don't touch the snooze alarm! Take your shower! YL and his father had done this same routine ever since his parents divorced and his dad had landed the job out in Cheyenne. YL missed his mom who lived in Detroit, and in the mornings, YL missed his father, but at least his father was only a voice away.

YL's bare feet shuffled across the cold linoleum in the hallway to the warm, fuzzy bathroom rug. He pulled the string connected to the solitary, dangling bathroom bulb. The room filled with eye-splitting brightness. YL blinked at his reflection in the mirror. He rubbed a hand over his short kinky black hair and stared at his round, buttonlike nose. He saw a piece of paper taped to his toothbrush. *Dear Favorite Son of Mine* was scrawled on the Scotch-taped note. YL laughed. "Of course I'm your favorite son," YL commented aloud. "I'm your *only* son, Dwayne," he answered as though his father were standing there in the bathroom instead of working at the radio station. YL read, *I'll be home at three-thirty*—and the smile on YL's face worked into an instant grin—*we have some shopping to do.* "Hot dog," he said. "Hot! Dog!" As the shower pipes clanked and clunked, Tina Turner's throaty voice belted out a verse of a song about a proud girl named Mary, from the radio in the next room.

* * *

"Hey, punkin face, what do you want for breakfast?" Evan Spagnolo asked his sister.

"Don't call me that, Evan," Sophie answered, setting her backpack on the kitchen chair. "I don't want anyone here to know that's my nickname. It's bad enough they call me Sophie the Sofa at school, and it's only my first week."

Evan looked at his sister. "Maybe you're a little on the plump side, but not fat. Punkin face is an endearing nickname. I gave it to you myself when you were just a baby." He took a box of cereal from the shelves of the small pantry beside the kitchen table. "What's it going to be?" he asked, holding up first one box, then the other. "Frosted Eyelashes? Or Toasted Toenails?"

"Toasted Toenails," Sophie replied, searching the silverware drawer for two teaspoons. "I sure wish Mom would buy some unhealthy kinds of cereals." Sophie made a face as she studied the list of ingredients for Frosted Eyelashes.

"Maybe we could get her to buy some of those new Chocolate Covered Earlobes advertised on TV," Evan suggested.

Sophie nodded, chewing a spoonful of cereal and watching her brother. He poured dry cereal into a bowl. He held it up in the air and checked the height. Sophie shook her head. He took two flakes, held the bowl up again, and then returned the two flakes to the cereal box.

"Now that's a perfect bowl of cereal," he said.

"You're crazy, you know it?"

"Yep," he replied. "It's what happens to you when you get to be a senior in high school. Seniors get a little weird around the edges, you know." He looked at her and crossed his eyes.

Five-year-old Lana skipped into the room, her shoelaces clinking on the floor.

"Over here, shortcake," Evan ordered.

Lana placed a sneakered foot on Evan's knee. He tied her shoe.

Sophie frowned. "If Evan keeps tying your shoes for you, Lana, you'll never learn how to do it yourself."

Lana turned away from Sophie's gaze and raised her eyebrows. "Don't be dumb, Sophie, that's why I'm in school. I can't graduate from Miss Cooke's kindergarten class unless I can count to one hundred by twos and tie my shoes."

Mrs. Spagnolo stepped into the kitchen. "So, tell me, girls, are you two just wowing the socks off everyone at the Whispering Springs Elementary School these days? Are both of you making tons and tons of new friends?"

Evan slid two slices of bread in the toaster for Lana.

"Heather MacIntosh invited me to her birthday party on Saturday," Lana replied, setting a jar of apricot jam on the table. "We're going to buy the present after school today, right, Mom?"

"Right, sweetie. How about you, punkin face? Have you made any friends yet? Have you had a chance to get to know the Briscoe children? Or the Lufflin girl?"

Mrs. Spagnolo asked. "I met their mothers at a room-mothers' meeting."

"I don't need to," Sophie replied between bites of cereal, although she didn't look up to see Evan's frown.

"Sophie, how can you say that? I really wish you'd try to make friends here," her mother urged.

"But, Mom," Sophie replied. "I already have Fiddle for a friend. I know I'll have a letter from her soon. I mailed a letter to her the day we got here." Sophie's best friend from Magnolia was one Mary Jane Ziels-dorf, also known as Fiddle because she started playing a miniature violin at age four. The Zielsdorfs and the Spagnolos had had backyards that touched. Sophie and Fiddle had been in diapers together, had learned how to walk together, and had been in the same classrooms from preschool to fifth grade.

Evan checked his watch. A loud buzzer sounded in the kitchen which signaled a customer was at the motel office.

"Oops, that must be the couple from Room Twenty-five checking out," Mrs. Spagnolo said, heading for the door.

Evan put his bowl and spoon in the sink. "Come on, troops, let's get this show on the road. Do you have your tutu for dance class this afternoon?" he teased Sophie.

"Evan!" Sophie complained. "How many times do I have to tell you? We don't wear tutus."

Evan picked up his stack of schoolbooks, balanced them under his right arm, then pirouetted in the middle of the kitchen floor.

"Evan!" Sophie shouted. "Mom," Sophie called, even though she knew her mother was in the motel office and couldn't hear her. Lana ignored them both, picked up her lunch box, and grabbed the two slices of toast off the plate as she walked out the door.

Evan took the keys to the station wagon from the hook by the kitchen telephone.

"Mom said this morning that she has all kinds of people checking out and Dad's working on the sign again, so I can have the car."

The cold morning air filled Sophie's lungs as she ran down the long sloping motel driveway. She waved to her father.

"Hey, Dad," she called. She stared at the sign her father was determined to fix. Cres Moo tel flashed intermittently.

"Have a good day, punkin face," her father called from his perch on the long stepladder. Sophie waved and ran to the mailbox, placing her letter to Fiddle inside.

"Write soon," Sophie said out loud, knowing Evan and Lana couldn't hear. Sophie turned the letter so the mailman wouldn't see the message she'd written on the back.

$$
\begin{array}{r r}
2 & \text{Good} \\
2 & \text{Be} \\
\hline
4 & \text{Gotten}
\end{array}
$$

Evan honked the horn, yelling, "Hey, Anna Pavlova, hustle your tutu. I want to get there early so I can watch Josie Baskim put her books in her locker!"

*   *   *

"Today, buying and selling take priority," Harper read aloud from her Junior Astrologer's Pocket Horoscope Forecaster. "Friends bring words of advice, if only you will take the time to listen," she continued, frowning. "What friends?" Harper asked Jupiter, her cat who was now curling around her ankles. "So tell me, Jupiter," she said, reaching down to scratch between her ears, "what friends? This is only my first week in school. How can I have friends already?" She tucked the pocket horoscope guide on the shelf by the telephone.

Meeeooow! Meeeooow!

"All right, Jupiter, I'll feed you."

The long-haired, black-and-white, splotchy-faced cat stretched against Harper's leg. Razorlike claws pierced the thin material of her pants.

"Yeeeooow!" Harper screeched. "I get your message," she said, pushing the cat aside. Harper began the morning ritual with Jupiter that they both knew so well.

"Here, Jupiter, watch your loving owner put the cat crunchies into the dish. Yum. Yum. See your devoted owner smoosh the cat food with a fork. MMMmmmm. Yummy, yummy, yummy." Harper turned the can to read the label. "Salmon supreme, darling. Your very favoritest flavor in the whole, wide world." She placed the saucer of food on the floor and the cat began a loud, steady *purrrrrrr. Purrrrrrr. Purrrrring* mixed with chomp-chomp-smacking sounds.

"I'll never understand how it is that a cat can purr and eat at the same time," Harper commented, half to herself, half to Jupiter.

Harper grabbed two toaster pastries from a box in the kitchen cabinets by the sink. She aimed the pastries at the toaster. They clunked into the slots. She slammed down the lever.

She picked up her backpack and tiptoed down the hallway toward her mother's bedroom. Open textbooks were strewn across her desk. A pair of high-top basketball shoes were tilted against the dresser. An orange-and-black jersey with the number 8 on it was draped over the back of a chair. The slightly opened door moved silently against Harper's light touch. Harper knew her mother had been studying for a big test. Her steady, sleep-filled breathing continued. She would sleep until noon, then head out for her afternoon and evening classes and basketball practice. Harper closed the bedroom door. She juggled the two pop-up pastries, shifting the hot rectangles from hand to hand. Leaning over the kitchen sink, she bit into the pink frosting of the pastry and picked up her fortune-telling, magic eight ball. She tipped the ball upside down and held it in that position while she thought to herself.

Will I finally find a real friend? she asked. A real, true-blue friend, now that we'll be staying in Whispering Springs for a while? She stopped to count the places she and her mother had called home since leaving Washington state. There was Utah, Oregon, Illinois, New York, and Wisconsin. Harper tipped the magic eight ball right side up, waiting for an answer to appear in the bubbly, blue water.

The blackish, bluish circle cleared. A whitish edge of a triangular shape touched the glass. Bubbles moved to the surrounding surface of the circle. The blue-lettered triangle floated flatly onto the glass. The magic eight ball predicted *Better Not Tell You Now.*

CHAPTER THREE

TNT

"**N**ew reading groups are posted on the back bulletin board," Mrs. TenBroeck explained on Monday morning. "I'll see the Gyroscopes at ten-thirty, the Zephyrs at ten-fifty, and the Labyrinths at eleven-ten."

Bobby Ray McKinnon shook his head and rolled his eyes. "Here we go again, can you believe the names she gives our reading groups?" he whispered to Sophie.

"Nope. I've never heard of any of those things."

"Make sure you look them up," Bobby Ray warned. "Old Tennie quizzes us on the meanings." He shook his head again. "When we first started school this year, I was in the Canis Majors," he said, shrugging. "When she tested me on it, I told her I thought it was a baseball league. Boy, did I ever get my head chewed off." He pointed toward the list on the back wall. "You'll have time to check out which reading group you're in during TNT."

"TNT? What's TNT?"

"TenBroeck's Nerve-Soothing Time," Harold Pon explained, overhearing the conversation. "It's when Tennie reads to us or else she makes everyone in the room read for thirty minutes. She lets us read anything we want as long as we READ! Comic books. The funny papers. The back of a cereal box. Anything. She plays classical music the whole time. Whatever you do, though, don't talk, or she threatens you within an inch of your life. Heck, Old Tennie herself even sits at her desk and reads. Big thick books, too."

Sophie cleared off her desk. "What's a Canis Major anyway?" she asked Bobby Ray after a few seconds.

"It sure ain't a baseball league; trust me, I learned the hard way. It's a bunch of stars," he told her, looking at the ceiling, "as in up in the sky," he finished.

During the TNT, Sophie checked the reading group lists posted on the wall.

GYROSCOPES	ZEPHYRS	LABYRINTHS
YL Truax	Rayna Abrams	Bobby Ray McKinnon
Sunday Margolis	Stephanie Grissom	Martin Jan
Sophie Spagnolo	Aloo Dubatti	Steve Coffinburger
Melody Briscoe	Sandra Lufflin	Charles Whiteside
Carnell Witherspoon	Harold Pon	Crosby Tull
Harper Lee Stritch	Amanda Washington	Emily Willcox
	Loren Oestergaard	Carla Clark
		Christa Billetts

When the class had finished reading during TNT, Mrs. TenBroeck closed her book and stood. "Do you know whose birthday it is this month, class?" A room filled with unblinking eyes stared at her. "I'll give you a hint," she encouraged, walking around the room between rows of desks, sometimes nudging a desk with her hip to straighten it. "We were listening to this composer today. We heard his Concerto for Piano and Orchestra No. Twenty-four in C Minor," she said, reading from the record label.

Students moved desks as Mrs. TenBroeck pointed to corners and edges, realigning metal legs with the antique floorboards. "All right. Here are your clues." She lifted her right hand, hummed a few bars of music, and directed an imaginary orchestra. "Clue number one, this composer has a January birthday." She looked around the room to see if anyone was going to venture an answer. "Moving right along, clue number two. He wrote his first symphony when he was only seven."

Charles Whiteside waved his hand in the air.

"Yes, Charles."

"Bay-toe-ven."

"No, sir," she replied, writing L-u-d-w-i-g v-a-n B-e-e-t-h-o-v-e-n on the board and looking for another volunteer.

"I know! I know!" Amanda Washington squealed. "Chi-cough-ski," she shouted.

"Peter Ilyich Tchaikovsky," Mrs. TenBroeck replied as she wrote. "Close, but no cigar. Let's try it again," she offered. She played the melody a second time.

YL Truax looked around the room. No one else was raising a hand. He slowly raised his hand halfway up, figuring Mrs. TenBroeck would miss it.

"Mr. Truax," she announced, walking toward him, "I knew I could count on you!"

"Mozart," he answered softly.

"YES!" she thundered. "Wolfgang Amadeus Mozart. Give this young man a round of applause and a Kewpie doll," she said, clapping her hands together. "Tell me, Mr. Truax, how it is that the son of a rock-and-roll disc jockey knows about Mozart's birthday?"

"My father plays lots of music at our house, Mrs. TenBroeck. He listens to all kinds of music; Mendelssohn, Bach, Thelonius Monk, Clark Terry, Art Blakey and the Jazz Messengers."

"What about rock and roll?"

"Not much rock and roll. Dad says rock and roll only pays the rent. His heart's really in jazz and classical music."

"I see."

"He played the flute in an orchestra, but now he plays with a jazz group on weekends when he has free time."

Mrs. TenBroeck stood beside YL's desk. She tapped it with her index finger.

"Mr. Truax, your father sounds like a very interesting person. Perhaps he'd be willing to come in this spring when I have career day and tell us what it is that he does."

YL nodded. The muscles in his shoulders relaxed once his teacher turned her back.

Explanations, explanations, explanations, YL thought. Why did moving to a new town always mean explaining everything to everyone all over again. YL watched as Mrs. TenBroeck moved over to Sophie's desk. He sighed. What a piece of luck that Mrs. Ten-Broeck hadn't asked about his mother. He hated having to explain that his parents were divorced.

"Miss Spagnolo," Mrs. TenBroeck asked, "do you know what time it is?"

"No, Mrs. TenBroeck."

"It's special story hour TNT time," Mrs. TenBroeck announced. "This time, *I'm* reading a novel to *you*." She took a book from a stack on the bookcase, then seated herself on the corner of her desk. She waited for students to put their work away.

"Open up those windows," Mrs. TenBroeck ordered. "I want the breeze blowing through here at a gale."

"But it's cold outside, Mrs. TenBroeck," Christa Billets replied, accidentally popping her gum. "It's January."

"That's exactly why I want them open, Christa. Deposit your gum in the wastebasket, please."

Crosby Tull, Emily Willcox, and Harper stepped up to the windows and muscled them open.

"I finished reading this over the weekend," Mrs. TenBroeck said, holding up the book and squinting at the spine. She put on her bifocals. *"Children of the Northern Lights*, by Edith Jana Franke." Mrs. TenBroeck pulled her skirt farther down on her knees. She held the book so the students could see a few of the pictures. She surveyed the room. "Get yourselves settled in," she advised. "I'm bound and determined to read you a chapter every time we have a break in the action." She looked around the room. "Are we ready, ladies and jelly beans?" She slid her bifocals farther down her nose and flipped through the first few pages.

Mrs. TenBroeck grew solemn. She looked up. "The dedication is taken from an Inuit song." She held the book high and in front of her face, yet her voice could be heard all the way in the back of the room.

Arise! Arise to meet the day.
As the first rays of morning's brightness fill the sky,
I search for the threads of light.
Gone is the dark of night.
Morning's welcome daylight shines across my face.
My eyes and heart greet a new dawn whitening the sky.

She turned the page and began looking around the room before she read.

Chapter One: In my dreams, the sun was shining. The hunting was good. I saw my father, Smoke Lying Close to the Ground, striding toward our igloo. "Aiyee!" he shouted to me, his face bright with happiness. "Aiyee!" Six plump fish swung from a pole balanced on his shoulder. Broken Smile, my mother, waved to him. "Aiyee," she called cheerfully. I could feel happiness in this dream of mine. And for the first time in many weeks, I could sense the happiness my parents shared.

"Fish for dinner," I cried. "Fish for dinner," I shouted, hurrying inside our igloo to tell Grandmother.

On this day, in my dreams, there would be no empty meat racks. No more empty stomachs. By firelight, in this dream of mine, my family ate a meal together. Father, Mother, Grandmother, Steps Softly, my baby sister, and me, a Netsilik child, by the name of Stars Beyond Counting. In this dream, Steps Softly watched me eat and laughed. Oh, the taste of that fish. In this dream of mine, there was the smell and feel of the meat against my tongue. Baby sister's cheeks glistened from the oily fish. And what a dream this was, the smell of food, the meat in my mouth—as real to me as they could be. Yet, this dream food stirred in me actual pangs of hunger, like the gnawing pains that my people had come to know so well. Our reality of a winter season with poor hunting, with no food and no prospects of game. This hunger encircled our lives, creeping into our stomachs, stealing silently, deeply into our chests. As I dreamed of swallowing the delicate bites of fish, tasting the meat in my mouth, I did what I had done night after night. I awoke.

Mrs. TenBroeck looked up, turning the page. The wind whipped snowflakes through the open windows. Goose bumps covered her bare arms. Students shivered. She continued:

Later that night, with the wind howling and snow pelting the side of our igloo, I heard my mother suddenly cry out in pain. The dim light of our soapstone lamp cast deep shadows across my father's worried face. He spoke softly to her. His voice touched my heart like a cold knife.

"What is it?" I asked.

"Quiet now," he cautioned. "Your mother is ill. I must take her to a doctor. I need your help, Stars Beyond Counting."

I looked up. "For what, Father?"

"To watch over our family. We must go, your mother and I."

"But the storm, Father."

Smoke Lying Close to the Ground shook his head. He watched Broken Smile's pale, motionless face as he spoke. "Her sickness knows nothing of storms. Grandmother has no more medicines. I must find a doctor." Father began packing small things into a pouch. "I fear that if we stay, your mother will die." By the firelight, I saw no softness in his expression, only the signs of concern and worry.

Outside our igloo, icy blasts of air swirled around my legs. Snow pellets stung my face as I watched Father carry Mother to the big sledge, lay her carefully onto the seat, and tuck a caribou skin around her. Mother never opened her eyes.

"Let me go with you?" I begged.

Father turned to me. "Stars Beyond Counting," he said sternly, "your work is here." He cracked his long whip over the dogs' heads and pulled away. We quickly waved.

Gusts of wind whistled past my ears. Snow beads beat on my back. A chill of cold air traveled along my arms and reached into my chest. Standing there in the half-light of afterdawn, a heaviness encircled me, since I knew I had become the keeper and head of our small family.

Mrs. TenBroeck closed the book.

"Now," she said, hopping off the desk, "I want you to do a couple of things. First of all, I want you to get into your reading groups." She began writing on the chalkboard, her bracelets jangling. "Gyroscopes, your job is to start a vocabulary list for this first chapter. I have a photocopy you can use. Zephyrs, you develop a list of characters and write a description of each. And, Labyrinths, I want you to begin drawing a group illustration for this chapter. I've stapled big sheets of paper on the back bulletin board." She waved her arm in the air. "Hustle, hustle. Let's get a move on. We've only got a few minutes before it's time to go home."

As the members of the Gyroscopes reading group moved to the back table, Melody went over to Carnell and Sunday Margolis and whispered something to them. The three took their seats at one end of the table, forcing Sophie, YL, and Harper to sit at the other end.

Mrs. TenBroeck brought the group the photocopied pages.

"I want a listing of your vocabulary words written on this chart paper," she told the group. "Sophie, why don't you and Melody write the words?" The teacher turned and headed toward the Labyrinths.

Carnell and Sunday flipped through the stapled papers.

A ruby-stoned ring with small gold ornaments caught Sophie's eye. "What's that?" she asked, pointing to the fourth finger of Melo's left hand.

"My Faith, Hope, and Charity ring," she answered.

"Gyroscopes Reading Group," Mrs. TenBroeck called out from across the room, "you're supposed to be writing a list of vocabulary words. Not Talking!"

"Dream," Sunday said. Sophie carefully printed the letters D-R-E-A-M.

Carnell looked at the first page of the story. "If someone could have a name like Smoke Lying Close to the Ground, I can imagine the name my parents would give me." Carnell looked up. "They'd call me Always Late for Supper."

"You don't suppose they eat raw fish, do you?" Sunday asked.

"Of course they do," Harper replied.

"Well, aren't we a Little Miss Know-It-All?" Melody said. "Did you learn that in Wisconsin, or what?"

"Igloo. Inuit. Caribou," YL added to the list.

Sophie's eyes drifted from the chart paper to Melo's ring. A small gold heart, a cross, and an anchor dangled from a tiny loop by the stone.

"Heart for hope. Cross for faith. Anchor for charity," Melo whispered, pointing to each of the miniature ornaments.

"Looks like a feather to me," Harper whispered. Melody ignored her.

"Is it a birthstone ring?" Sophie asked.

"Geez, Sofa, don't be dumb," Melo said, without looking up. "It's our club ring. Everybody who belongs has one."

Sophie's Magic Marker made a blob on the T as it rested on the final letter of the word Inuit. She lifted her head. "Can I get a ring?" she asked.

"It's a *club*," Melo whispered, not all that softly. "You can't get a ring unless you're *invited* to be in the FAITH, HOPE, AND CHARITY CLUB."

"Who's in the club?"

"Me and some other girls. Suki Lufflin. Christa Billetts."

"Sandra Lufflin's in the club?"

"Nobody calls her Sandra. But, yeah, didn't I just say that?"

"Yes, but . . . Suki never asked me if I wanted to . . ." Sophie paused for a second. "I only . . ." She suddenly stopped speaking. She sensed a presence behind her. Before she knew it, Mrs. TenBroeck's firm hand was on her shoulder.

"Dream. Igloo. Inuit. Caribou," Mrs. TenBroeck read from Sophie's paper. "Keep going, Gyroscopes," she commented. "More writing than talking, please. I don't want to have to come back here again and speak to you all." The six students looked at their teacher. "A good vocabulary list takes some thinking. I said to put your heads together, not hold a cocktail party back here."

The group resumed their work, but Sophie's

thoughts drifted off the assignment. How come Suki Lufflin had never once mentioned the Faith, Hope, and Charity Club? Hadn't Suki and Sophie walked to dance class together? Hadn't Evan given Suki a ride home from class last Thursday afternoon? So how come Suki hadn't asked Sophie to belong?

Sophie's stomach began to ache. At first the pain was small, like the size of a quarter, but the more she thought about walking back and forth to dance class, the bigger and sicker the feeling in her stomach became. She'd never in a million years thought that being new would feel so awkward. How come she was having to ask everyone how to do things? Wasn't she the new kid? Hadn't her mother said that the students at Whispering Springs would take Sophie under their wing? Sophie shook her head. "No one's taking me under their wing, that's for sure," she muttered to herself.

"What did you say?" Carnell asked.

"It's all bird dookey," Sophie answered.

"Bird dookey?" he repeated, giving her a puzzled look. "You're weird," he replied.

"Class." Mrs. TenBroeck's voice brought Sophie's thoughts to an abrupt halt. "It's time to get ready to go home. The bell is about to ring."

Students scurried, gathering papers together, stuffing books into their desks, scuffling their feet. Bam! Bam! Desk lids slammed all over the room.

Children retrieved their belongings from the cloakroom and lined up in the front of the room.

"The word for tomorrow," Mrs. TenBroeck announced, looking over the parade of students, "is kamiks."

"Kamiks?" Aloo Dubatti repeated.

"Kamiks," Mrs. TenBroeck confirmed, "K-A-M-I-K-S. Go home tonight and ask your mothers if they know what kamiks are. Inuit mothers play an important role with kamiks." She turned and shooed the line of children out the door.

YL lagged a little behind the others.

"Mrs. TenBroeck, I don't have a mother at home to ask." He hesitated before he continued. "My mother lives in Detroit," he explained.

"You could ask your father, then," Mrs. TenBroeck suggested.

YL nodded and followed Bobby Ray, Crosby, and Steve Coffinburger through the doorway.

Sophie walked beside Harper. "I bet my dad will know what kamiks are. How about yours?"

"My dad is dead."

"You mean really dead?"

"Yeah, he's *really* dead. I wouldn't kid about something like that. He died in Vietnam when I was a little kid."

"That's sad," Sophie said, standing close enough to Harper to see the fine spray of freckles across her nose and cheeks. Small, pierced, crescent-moon earrings hung to the bottom of Harper's straight, jet-black hair.

"My uncle died in Vietnam, too," Bobby Ray said, overhearing their conversation. "His name is on the wall they built for the soldiers in Washington. My aunt Ginnie went down there and saw it for herself. I never met my uncle; I was only a little baby when he died. They named me Bobby Ray, after him."

"That's the same with me. My mom said my father went to fight in Vietnam, but he never came back," Harper replied. "Now, it's only my mom and me."

Sophie thought of her mother at the motel and her father up on the ladder, fixing the sign. "I think I'd really hate not having a dad."

"I do. I think it would be nicer to have two parents. It's me and my mom and our cat," Harper said.

YL and the three boys rushed past them.

"You ever heard of kamiks?" Bobby Ray asked.

"Nope," YL said.

"Sometimes I think she makes up the words just to drive us nuts. You know what I mean?" Crosby offered.

"Wouldn't surprise me," Steve replied.

The boys leaped down the steps near the office.

"Kamiks," YL repeated. "What do you suppose they are?"

"Beats me. But I'm not going to waste my time looking it up. Amanda Washington always has the answers to everything. Bet you a quarter she's got the answer tomorrow morning," Harold suggested.

"You're on! Aiyee!" Crosby yelled as they jumped off the last two steps. YL stopped and watched the other boys heading over to the football field in the park. He thought about asking if he could join them, but decided against it. Instead, he walked to the end of the block, turned down Benson Avenue, and used the key around his neck to let himself into his apartment.

"Dad?" he called out, but the only thing that greeted him was the empty echo of his own voice.

CHAPTER FOUR

Missions

Headlights from the school bus flashed over the top of the hill.

"Hurry up, Sophie, here comes the bus," Lana called into the chill morning air. First the lights on the bus flashed yellow, then switched to red.

Click. Flash. Click. Flash. Click. Flash. The STOP sign flapped into position beside the driver's window as Sophie reached the bottom of the driveway. As predictable as clockwork, bus #128 came to a screeching halt along the highway by the long drive leading up to the motel at precisely 7:49 A.M.

Lana climbed aboard.

"Good morning, Lana."

"Hi, Mr. Duke."

"Good morning, Sophie," said the driver. Lana ran down the aisle and scooted into a seat beside Heather MacIntosh. "And how's every little thing this morning, girls?"

Sophie smiled. "Fine, Mr. Duke. How about your-self?" she returned.

"Couldn't be better." He pulled on the lever to close the door, flipped the handle for the STOP sign, and flicked the switch for the flashing lights. "Couldn't be better."

The bus lurched forward and picked up speed, then made a U-turn at the Davistown Road intersection and passed by the motel again on its trip to Whispering Springs Elementary.

Sophie waited for Mr. Duke to tell her a corny joke, as he'd done every morning since the first day of school. "So tell me, Sophie, what did the wallpaper say to the wall?"

Sophie settled into a seat in the second row. She thought for a second. "I don't know, Mr. Duke. What did the wallpaper say to the wall?"

He looked into the mirror, grinning as the bus bounced along. "Stick 'em up, I've got you covered."

"That's a good one, Mr. Duke," Sophie said, look-ing over at the radio. "Could you tune into WMTN this morning, Mr. Duke?"

"Sure thing," he said, flicking another knob. Static greeted them as he flipped through the stations.

A verse of the song, *Monday, Monday,* drifted out over the bus speakers.

"Good Monday morning again, everyone. Time to get that ice scraped off your windshield. Better button up your jacket. It's a chilly twenty-one degrees in Mor-gantown. And all you kiddiewinkers on your way to

*school this morning, you have a good day, you hear?
This is your old buddy, Dwayne, the Dynamo, Truax
wishing you a super day. And the rest of you folks out
there in radio land, keep your radio dial tuned to 91.6,
for W M T N, West Virginia's best, rock-* [babies waaa-
hed] *and-* [a chorus of dogs barked] *roll* [race cars
revved their engines] *station. The time at the tone is
eight o'clock. State and local news is next. . . ."*

As the bus pulled into the school parking lot, Sophie
spotted Harper walking into the building. YL stood
beside the door.

Sophie jumped off the bus and hurried toward the
building. "Hey, Harper," she called out.

"Hey, YL," the two girls said at exactly the same
time.

"Jinx," Harper said quickly. Sophie laughed. She
hadn't heard that expression since she'd left Delaware.

"We listened to your dad on the radio this morning," Sophie said.

"Yeah? Me, too. I hear him every morning. Here,"
YL replied, handing two small envelopes to Sophie
and Harper as they walked past him.

They ripped open the envelopes and read:

YOU'RE INVITED TO A BIRTHDAY PARTY!
Place: Little Italy Pizza Parlor
Time: 5:30 P.M. Date: This Saturday
Birthday Celebration for: YL Truax

*   *   *

Crosby pulled a quarter out of his pants pocket and laid it on Harold Pon's desk as Amanda Washington spieled off the meaning of kamiks.

"Didn't I tell you? She's a walking encyclopedia," Harold whispered. Everyone in the room listened to Amanda's scratchy voice reading the dictionary definition.

"Kamiks," she whined, holding the piece of notebook paper within an inch of her nose. "Boots made by Eskimos from the skins of animals, generally a combination of polar bear, seal, and caribou." Amanda looked up for Mrs. TenBroeck's approval.

"I'll make one correction, citizens of Room Seventeen. The word Eskimo is sometimes considered a derogatory term. I would prefer that you use the term Inuit when you are referring to native people from the Arctic region. Thank you, Amanda."

"Told you so," Harold whispered to YL. Harold balanced the quarter on its edge and gave it a twirl. He watched it silently spin.

Mrs. TenBroeck opened up one of the side cupboards next to her desk and pulled out what looked like a coat. She began to unfold it, then carefully draped it around her shoulders.

"We're continuing part of our social studies unit this morning by looking at Inuit dress," she explained, strolling around the room with the heavy fur coat hanging over her shoulders. "I brought in this caribou jacket my father and I found on one of our trips to Alaska a few years ago." She walked between the rows of desks and held open the coat so the students could touch the soft fur. "This particular coat was made by Enook Kisik from Frobisher Bay. Can you see the special pattern along the cuffs?" She stretched out her arms so that everyone could see the beaded design. She walked past Harper's desk.

"It's so soft," Harper said, touching a corner, "like my cat's fur."

"Yes, and warm, too," Mrs. TenBroeck replied. "Aloo, will you get the lights for me, please?" The teacher walked to the back of the room, clicking on a slide projector. The big white screen in front of the chalkboard was immediately filled with a landscape scene that looked nothing like Whispering Springs. Jagged, snow-covered mountains. Clear blue sky. "We saw long stretches of tundra. Roads that seemed to never end." Mrs. TenBroeck kept tapping the remote control of the slide projector. "This next slide is of a man working on a totem pole. Do you know the purpose behind totem poles?" She looked around the room.

Emily Willcox raised her hand. "Are they like street signs?"

"Well, in a way, Emily, but there's something else."

The class turned toward Amanda Washington, who only shrugged.

"A totem pole signifies . . ." Mrs. TenBroeck began.

Sophie stared at the design. She liked the faces that looked like masks, the colors, the clear cuts in the woods . . . then, something touched her arm. She turned. Suki Lufflin handed her a note as Mrs. Ten-Broeck's voice started to describe totem poles in other parts of Alaska and Canada.

Do you want to be in FH + C? the message asked.

Sophie looked up. Melody and Suki were watching her. Sophie nodded her head, yes. Harper saw, too, and frowned.

"Meet us by the bookstore after lunch," Melo said, leaning across Bobby Ray's row.

"Melody Briscoe, stop talking," Mrs. TenBroeck commanded, without even turning around to see who it was. She clicked another slide. The entire class began to laugh. There, on the screen, was a picture of a much younger Mrs. TenBroeck in flashy sunglasses and an enormous, gilt-edged blue sombrero, a serape draped over one shoulder. She was feeding a carrot to a donkey who was also wearing a sombrero.

"Line up for lunch," she ordered quickly. "How on earth did that ever get in there?" she remarked, fumbling for the on/off switch.

Harper stood next to Sophie in the girls' room while they washed their hands.

"Why do you want to be in their dumb old club, anyway?"

Sophie looked up. "How did you know?"

"I heard about it the very first day I got here," Harper bragged, trying to make it sound as though she really had. "You couldn't pay me to be in it."

Sophie didn't know what to say. They'd already asked

Harper? Before they'd asked Sophie? She dried her hands with one of the scratchy, brown paper towels.

"They'll make you do dumb stuff," Harper warned, taking a towel. She wiped her hands, crumpling the towel into a ball and tossing it into the center of the trash can. "Two points," she announced.

Sophie ignored Harper's basket. "What do you mean, dumb stuff?"

"Like eat a whole jar of pickled herring, or something gross like that. Or maybe even go outside in your underwear and mail a letter."

"How do you know?"

"Because there was a club like that in Kenosha."

"Were you in it?"

"I started to be, but they wanted me to do some even dumber stuff, so I quit."

"I don't think they'll make me do dumb stuff. My mom says Suki Lufflin comes from a very nice family."

"Oh, right. Nice family, baloney. Just wait and see. They'll make you do dumb stuff."

"Well, nobody can *make* me do anything I don't want to do."

Harper frowned. "Yeah, right." She pointed her finger at Sophie. "Don't forget those famous last words when you're standing out by a big blue United States mailbox in your panties and training bra."

Sophie watched Harper walk away from her. She looked at the clock in the hallway. Only one more hour until lunch.

*   *   *

The crisp five-dollar bill that had started out in Sophie's pocket at eight o'clock in the morning was now a crumpled wad.

"What's this?" Mrs. Ortni asked at the bookstore as Sophie put the green lump on the counter. "Is it still legal tender?"

"I'd like one of those big boxes of new crayons," Sophie said, remembering to add "please" an instant before it was too late.

"Don't worry, we only sell new crayons here, Sophie," Mrs. Ortni remarked. She lifted the lid. She and Sophie admired the waxy-smelling crayons. The older woman held up a crayon and took off her glasses to read the label. "This one, carnation pink, is my favorite color. How about you?"

"Periwinkle is mine," Sophie explained. "My little sister Lana has been wanting a box of these for her birthday. If I hide them here at school, she won't get her little mitts on them until this weekend."

"Does she like to draw?"

"Yes, ma'am. She does, and I really do, too."

Mrs. Ortni smiled and handed Sophie her change.

"Let's make sure none of those crayons spill out," she said, stretching two wide rubber bands around the box.

"Thanks," Sophie said, beaming.

"You're welcome, honey. Bring me back a picture sometime."

Sophie stepped away from the door of the bookstore to find Melody and Suki coming down the hall.

"What'd you buy?" Melo asked.

"Crayons."

"Crayons? Aren't you too old for crayons?"

"No, they're a birthday present for my sister. I'm going to hide the box here at school, then she'll never find them."

Suki shifted restlessly from one foot to another. She elbowed Melody.

"So, Sofa," Melo began to say, "do you want to know about being in the Faith, Hope, and Charity Club or what?"

"Sure."

"Okay, here's how it works." Melody looked up and down the hallway. "We have to talk about the missions you're going to go on first, to see whether or not you can join."

"Missions?" Sophie asked.

"Yeah, missions," Suki replied sassily.

"What missions?" Sophie asked.

The laughter of teachers could be heard coming from the teachers' lounge.

"Come on, let's get out of here so we can talk," Melody suggested.

"Yeah, let's get out of here," Suki echoed.

"You want me to do *what?*" Sophie nearly shouted, standing on the stairs to the rear entrance of the cafeteria.

"Take it easy, Sophie. Don't pop a gut. Besides mailing this letter to me in your underwear, we *only* want you to take Steve Coffinburger's glass eye." Melody handed Sophie a mint-green envelope with a stamp already in the right-hand corner. The mission with the letter was somewhat understandable, but the eyeball mission didn't make sense to Sophie.

"*Only* take his glass eye?" Sophie repeated.

Melody turned to Suki. "Wasn't that what I said, Suki? Yeah, we want you, Sophie the Sofa Spagnolo, to take Steve Coffinburger's glass eye."

"You mean steal it out of his desk?"

"No, dummy, out of his head while he's wearing it." Melody frowned. "Look at it this way, Sophie, the club considers it *borrowing*. All the members of the club want to do is get a chance to look at it in private."

"Hey, Sofa, don't come unglued here. It's only borrowing," Suki added.

"I didn't even know he *had* a glass eye."

"Yeah, well he does," Melody explained. "Just *borrow* it during last recess, and you can put it back in his desk before he comes in the next morning."

"See, I told you it was only borrowing," Suki reassured Sophie.

"What if he needs it?"

"He won't, it's his spare," Melody added when Sophie looked surprised. "Yeah, he's got a spare eyeball. See, we've all watched him take the spare out of his desk, but he'll only show it to the boys in the class. That's why we want *you* to *borrow* it so that the girls in the club can see it, too," Melody said.

"Well, I don't know," Sophie replied, shaking her head. "What if I get caught? What happens if I drop it. I'm a butterfingers sometimes."

Melody took a step closer to Sophie. "Listen, Sofa, do you want to be in the club or not?"

"I think so."

Melody put her face right up to Sophie's. "Then you've got to take this first step. You've got to go on the missions."

Sophie looked from Suki to Melody, and back again. Suddenly, she heard her mother's voice inside her head: *Sophie, I really wish you'd try to make friends.*

"Okay," she answered.

"Come on, let's get out of here," Suki ordered.

Sophie held up the box of crayons.

"If you wait a minute while I put these in my desk, I'll go outside to recess with you, Suki."

"Not today," she replied, halfway out the door.

"After you're in the club," Melo said.

"Oh," Sophie answered, "okay."

Sophie opened the lid of the new box of crayons and took one sniff of the waxy smell before she tucked the box deep into her desk. She grabbed her dance-class bag from the hook in the cloak closet and tucked the envelope inside. As she walked out of the room, she looked at Steve Coffinburger's desk. It was behind Aloo's and in front of Martin Jan's.

"What have I gotten myself into," she muttered nervously thinking of the envelope, then remembering the eyeball. "If this is what it takes," she started to say aloud, hoping to give herself some encouragement, "then tomorrow, I guess I'm going to *borrow* an eyeball."

CHAPTER FIVE

Sixth-Grade Bag of Nerves

"Once we've heard the next chapter in *Children of the Northern Lights*, we're going to work on something special," Mrs. TenBroeck announced after recess. "Ready?" she asked, scooting onto the corner of her desk. "Christa, you can take off your coat, I'm not going to keep the windows open today while I read." Mrs. TenBroeck cleared her throat, positioned her glasses on the end of her nose, and placed the bookmark on her desk.

Chapter Two: The light of day would not come for many hours, and so I removed my clothes and crawled between the warm layers of caribou bedding. Steps Softly slept peacefully next to Grandmother. Apoppa and Tiintuk, my dogs, were safe in their special shelter from the storm. Half dreaming, half waking, I waited and hoped for the storm to subside so that I could go out and hunt for the food I knew we would need to survive the next few days.

The passage of time, the measure of our Netsilik lives, is determined by the stars and moon. One snow-blinding day can easily melt into the next or into many. The blowing storm and driving snow had kept me from checking the moon, but I knew the importance of keeping track of the time now that my father and mother were gone. I turned on my side. Using mother's ulu, I chipped one chink into the snow-block wall of our igloo, counting the days, First, one. One day without my parents.

Steps Softly moved under her layers of covers. Grandmother drew her closer for warmth. I carefully concentrated on watching the spot in our igloo where Father had stretched a pane of bearded sealskin to frame a window and let in light. I checked the moss wick of the lamp to make sure it would keep burning. Mother was very skilled and could keep three lamps burning at once.

Stay awake, I whispered. Do not fall asleep, I thought. The wind howled and screeched. Strong gusts blew from the north. Would the storm ever subside?

I lay there in the warm layers of bedding and formed a plan. I would recite all the stories and songs Grandmother had taught me to keep myself awake. That way I could tend our soapstone lamp, our only source of light and heat. As I recalled Grandmother's favorite story, I heard her familiar voice telling this tale.

There once was an enormous bear, who was so large that he carried on his back a sack filled with all the winds of the world. Only the bear could open this heavy bag, but every hunter who met him was most curious. "Tell us what is in your sack," they pleaded. "I am carrying a load of rock," the bear answered. "Now go away and do not bother me." But one hunter did not follow the bear's orders. The sly hunter tracked the bear for many days and nights. One night after the deceitful hunter sang the bear to sleep with a long and sad song, the hunter stole the bear's sack and opened it. The hunter was immediately thrown to the ground as something huge and fierce escaped from the bear's bag. The winds of the world roared onto the earth, escaping north, south, east, and west, farther than the eye could see, more distant than the ear could hear. The winds of the world howled. The winds of the world screeched and moaned, trying to fill the mighty spaces on the earth with gusts and breezes and gales of frigid air. The hunter pleaded with the bear, "Oh, powerful bear, you can have anything of mine you wish. Only take back your wind." But the hunter's generous offer mattered not to the bear. He answered by shaking his large furry head. There was not one earthly thing of the thieving hunter's the bear wanted. And the wise bear also knew that there was nothing he could recover, since the north, south, east, and west winds had entered the world for all time.

At that instant, a chilling draft of air entered our igloo, causing the flame to flicker. Watch the flame, I repeated. Watch the flame. My eyelids grew heavy. I listened to the voice of the wind. It whistled a strong, steady, icy song from the north. *Woooo-eee. Wooooeee. Woooo-eee.* And before I could help myself, I had fallen asleep.

Mrs. TenBroeck closed the book and set it on her lap.

"Well my little polar bears. What do you think's going to happen?" She looked around the room as students raised their hands. "Aloo?"

"I think the lamp is going to go out," she answered.

"Naw, I think the grandmother's going to wake up and save the day," Martin shouted out.

"Fair enough," Mrs. TenBroeck said, hopping down from the desk. "Here's what we're going to do next. Remember the poems we wrote before Christmas? What were they called, class?"

Students called out, "Cinquains!"

"And how many lines did they have?"

"Five!"

"And how were they set up?" Mrs. TenBroeck asked, standing by the chalkboard, chalk in hand.

"Title, describe title, action, action, action, feeling about the title, title," the class answered in unison.

Mrs. TenBroeck smiled and wrote the format on the chalkboard.

"And now, my intrepid sled dogs, what do you think I'm going to ask you to do next?"

"Write a cinquain!" the students answered.

"My goodness, aren't we sharp as a tack today? Yes, my little kumquats, I want you to get into your reading groups and write a group cinquain about what you've heard so far. Something to do with the story or the characters. All you need to take is a piece of paper, pencil, and your brain. Zephyrs, up here. Labyrinths, you go in the middle, there," Mrs. TenBroeck said, pointing to a cluster of desks in the center of the room. "Gyroscopes, back to the reading table."

Sophie, YL, and Harper straggled to their places.

"Have you ever done one of these before?" Sophie asked Harper.

"Nope, I've never even heard of cinquains."

"They're easy," Carnell explained. "What should we make the title?"

"How about 'Stars Beyond Counting'?" YL offered. Carnell began writing.

"Then describe the title," Sunday said. "How about Inuit."

"And maybe add protector," Sophie added.

"Not so fast," Carnell complained. "I can't get everything written down."

"Let's put hunting, for one of the action words," Melody said.

"Surviving," Harper added.

"And sleeping," Sunday finished.

Carnell scribbled the words on the paper.

"How about 'caretaker of the lamp' for the next line," YL said.

"Yeah, I like that," Carnell added.

"Hey, Carnell, instead of protector, why don't we put Boy, so that it says Inuit, Boy, on the second line," Melody suggested. "I think protector sounds wimpy."

Sophie sat silently.

"Boy? Why would we want to put Boy?" Harper asked. "Stars Beyond Counting is a girl."

Melody looked up quickly. "You've got to be kidding me. It says right there in the story that Stars Beyond Counting is a boy."

"Where? Where does it say that?" Harper countered. "Show me."

Mrs. TenBroeck made a swing past the Gyroscopes. "Do I hear the faint sounds of dissension? I love a good, hot debate!"

Melody pointed to Harper. "Little Miss Encyclopedia, here, says that Stars Beyond Counting is a girl. Tell Harper, Mrs. TenBroeck, that it says right in the story . . ."

"It says where?" the teacher interrupted.

"Well, doesn't it say that Stars is a boy in the beginning when his father's walking toward their igloo carrying the fish?" YL asked.

"Unless my eyes are failing me, I don't believe it does," Mrs. TenBroeck answered.

"Doesn't it say that Stars is a boy when the father leaves and tells him that he's in charge of the family?" Sunday asked.

Mrs. TenBroeck shook her head, no.

"I mean, it's too stupid to think that a father would leave and tell his *daughter* that she was in charge of the family, isn't it? Girls don't do stuff like that," Melody said.

"Oh, really?" Mrs. TenBroeck answered, looking over her bifocals. "Why not?"

"Does it say anyplace that Stars is a *girl* or a *boy*?" Sophie questioned.

"Actually, Sophie, you're the closest to the truth,"

Mrs. TenBroeck replied. "As far as we've read in the story, I'm quite sure that Stars isn't identified as a boy or a girl." The teacher looked at the group. "Since we seem to have a modicum of disparity among the Gyroscopes for the moment, why don't you try this?" she offered. "Why don't each of you write a separate cinquain for the story. That way, you all won't have to agree on whether or not Stars is a girl or a boy."

Carnell nodded. YL began to write. Sunday chewed on the end of her pencil. Sophie looked at the board, and Melody Briscoe glared at Harper.

The 3:10 bell rang. Class was dismissed. Harper went home to feed Jupiter. YL's dad picked him up after school, then the two of them drove to the mall to buy birthday hats and party favors. And walking over to dance class, Sophie composed a cinquain about herself.

Title:	Sophie, the Sofa, Spagnolo
Describe title:	Sixth-grade bag of nerves
Action, Action, Action:	Walking, Dancing, Stealing
Feeling about the Title:	Reluctant eyeball thief
Title:	Sophie, the Sofa, Spagnolo

Miss Natalie's Ballet and Tap Dancing School was on the corner of West Third and Babcock streets. In the apartment above the dance studio, Harper stood in the shadows by the kitchen window watching students being dropped off for class. As Suki Lufflin shuffled along the sidewalk, Harper held back a corner of the curtain and ducked to one side.

Jupiter jumped onto the sink and walked across the drainboard to the window ledge. Harper spotted Sophie coming down the sidewalk, a block or so behind Suki. Jupiter pushed back the curtain just at the moment that Sophie looked up at the window, and Harper reached for her cat. Sophie saw Harper and smiled. They waved. Harper ran down the steps and out the door.

"What are you doing up there?" Sophie asked.

"It's where I live," Harper replied.

"It's a house?"

"No, an apartment, for me and my mom."

The girls looked up at the window as Jupiter tiptoed around the plants along the windowsill. They could see the cat's mouth meowing but couldn't hear anything.

"Is that your cat?"

Harper nodded.

"I love cats," Sophie said, "but we can't have one because my dad's allergic to them. He has these wicked sneezing fits whenever he gets around one. Can I come up after class and see her?"

"Sure."

"Your mom won't mind?"

"Nope, my mom is over at school, anyway. So it's only me and Jupiter for dinner."

"Okay, I'll stop by for a minute. Maybe Miss Natalie will get one of her tension headaches and let us out early."

CHAPTER SIX

Hello, Dearie

When dance class ended early, Sophie stepped around a tiny, white-haired woman wearing a lavender shawl. She was retrieving her mail in the hallway near the stairs to the apartments above the dance studio. "Hello, dearie," the elderly woman chirped. Sophie smiled and took the steps two at a time. As she knocked on Harper's door, her friend called out, "Come on in, I'm in the middle of making dinner."

"Your mom lets you cook?" Sophie asked, looking around the corner of the hallway and into the kitchen.

"Sure, I've been cooking since I was little," Harper replied, stirring a pan of macaroni and cheese on a front burner of the small stove. She dumped a can of green beans into a saucepan, then sliced two hot dogs, leaving them on the cutting board.

Sophie picked up Jupiter. The cat snuggled into the crook of her arm. Sophie ran her fingers through the soft fur on Jupiter's stomach. The cat purred and purred. Sophie looked around the room. Lush green plants crowded every windowsill, and pots of plants hung from hooks in the ceiling. A poster with Albert Einstein's grandfatherly face hung on the wall by the kitchen table. A small wooden shelf under another window held an assortment of books. Sophie glanced at the spines: *Charlotte's Web, To Kill a Mockingbird, Anne of Green Gables,* and *Know Your Constellations* was next to a book titled *Magical Children* and a copy of *Quick Fixes for Basic Household Repairs.*

"When does your mom get home?" Sophie asked, looking at papers strewn across the top of the kitchen table. Small pamphlets along with clippings from the newspaper lay by a set of silverware and a dinner plate. Jupiter squirmed out of Sophie's arms, landing on the couch.

"Mom has basketball practice this afternoon. She's the team manager," Harper said proudly. "Then she has philosophy class, and there's a Scramble so I don't expect her home until nine-thirty or ten."

"What's a Scramble? You mean you're here by yourself?"

"It's a pickup basketball game. And what's so weird about being here by myself? Miss McP lives across the hall, if I need anything. Besides, I'm not really alone. Jupiter's here."

"Jupiter's only a cat."

Harper looked at Jupiter, who was now asleep, upside down, between two fringed pillows on the couch.

"Jupiter, did you hear that insult? Sofe said you were *only* a cat!"

Jupiter never moved a muscle.

"Do you want some dinner? You're welcome to stay."

"No," Sophie answered, stepping up to the window and pulling back the curtain, "my brother will be here any minute."

Harper took a plate and a saucer from the cupboard and set them on the counter by the stove.

"What'd they tell you that you had to do?"

"Pardon me?"

"What'd they tell you that you had to do? Melo and Suki took you aside, didn't they, and told you about the dumb stuff you had to do to join the club, right?"

Sophie looked out the window. She didn't want to say too much.

"Sort of."

Harper added the hot-dog pieces to the macaroni and cheese.

"That smells so good," Sophie said, stepping over to the stove. Harper hopped onto a small step stool and stirred the macaroni and cheese with a vengeance. Pieces of cheesy elbow macaroni flipped out of the pan. Sophie picked them up with her fingers and popped them into her mouth.

"Sure you don't want to stay and eat with me?"

"No, Evan should be here any minute."

"They asked you to do something, didn't they?" Harper persisted.

Sophie turned away from the stove and looked at the booklets on the table, avoiding Harper's look. *Palm and Fingerprint Reading Made Easy. Predict the Future by the Stars. Astrology for Beginners.*

"Is this your mom's stuff?"

"No, it's mine," Harper answered, dishing spoons full of macaroni and cheese onto two plates. She set one plate on the floor for Jupiter. The cat scampered off the couch. Harper drained the steaming green beans and spooned a few onto her plate. "Here," she offered, drying her hands on the apron she was wearing and picking up a round black ball. "Have you got a burning question to ask?" she said, handing the black ball to Sophie.

Sophie inspected it. "Well, maybe," she replied. "What is this?"

"It's a magic eight ball. You ask it questions," Harper told her. "You can ask the magic eight ball anything you want. I ask it stuff all the time." Harper set the ball down. Sophie continued staring at it. "It gives you answers. Don't worry, it's not going to levitate."

"What's levitate?"

"Lift off, you know, rise up." Harper set her plate on the table and pulled out a chair. She seated herself and flapped open a cloth napkin.

"Oh."

"Ask away," Harper said, stabbing at some macaroni, two green beans, and a slice of hot dog with her fork.

"Do I have to ask out loud?"

"Not if you don't want to. I can plug my ears, if you like."

"Okay."

Sophie held the ball for a minute. Harper gripped her fork in one hand and put her index fingers up to her ears.

The black surface of the eight ball was shiny. The circle with the squarish number eight in the center made it look like a billiard ball from a pool table. Sophie closed her eyes, then mumbled to herself, "Should I go on a mission so I can be in the Faith, Hope, and Charity Club?"

"Ha!" Harper spluttered, green beans tumbling out of her mouth. She covered her mouth with her hand.

"You cheated! You listened!" Sophie said.

The two girls smiled at the same time. Sophie flipped over the magic eight ball and waited for her answer.

Reply Hazy, Try Again, the ball displayed.

A car honked outside.

"That must be Evan," Sophie said, returning the ball to Harper. "Thanks."

"You're welcome," Harper replied. "Come back again."

Sophie headed toward the door. She looked around the room and liked the way everything felt so friendly, so easy.

"Come when you can stay for dinner," Harper said, standing up, "and meet my mother."

"Okay, you're on," Sophie answered, stomping down the steps. "See you tomorrow," she called from the hallway below. "Maybe you could come out to the motel sometime." She turned to wave. "Don't do anything I wouldn't, Jupiter," Sophie shouted. Before she climbed into the backseat of the station wagon, she looked up at the window and laughed. Harper, holding Jupiter, was madly waving good-bye with the cat's paw.

"So far," YL told his father over a Texas hot dog at Mousey's Burger and Fry Stand that night during dinner, "they've guessed that my name is Yoo Landa and Yahoo Lunch!" He took a bite of his hot dog, then waved his hand in front of his mouth to cool off the effects of the spicy chili sauce.

Dwayne Truax dunked a french fry into a little white cup filled with ketchup. "So, what did you tell them?" he asked with a grin.

"What I always tell them."

"Which is nothing, right?" Dwayne replied.

"Right."

"You know, I gave you the initials of your name after one of my idols," his father explained.

"How come you used initials and didn't give me a name? Something regular like Dave or Steve or Jeff." YL took another bite of hot dog, chewed, and then washed it down with a sip of milk.

"Your mother and I thought you should have a name that would stand out."

YL's eyes widened. "It stands out, all right. I'll spend the rest of my life explaining what it isn't." He bit into a french fried onion ring and the long slippery onion slid out, clinging to his chin.

Dwayne Truax sprinkled more salt on his french fries, cautiously watching his son. "I'm afraid I have to talk to you about something that's not going to make you a happy camper."

YL felt his heart drop into his stomach.

"Oh, no, Dad. Don't do this to me. Don't tell me we've got to move again."

"Not, it's not that bad," his father explained. "Although it's not exactly going to be easy." Dwayne Truax took his napkin and wiped his hands. "They're changing my hours at work, and they're going to put me on nights."

"Every night? Geez louise, Dad."

"No, not every night, just Fridays and Saturdays."

"I'll never see you," YL said in disbelief.

"That's only half of the problem."

YL looked up quickly. He began shaking his head before he spoke. "Oh, no, Dad, don't do this to me. Don't make me have a baby-sitter. I'm too big, Dad, please, a million times. Don't make me have some little old lady come over and crochet while I watch TV. I'm a big kid, Dad. I can take care of myself. I know I can."

Dwayne Truax shook his head. "That isn't it, YL. I simply can't have you staying alone by yourself at night. I'm going to be working the eleven to seven shift."

"But I'll be asleep."

"I know you will, but I can't leave you alone."

YL put more mustard on his hot dog. "Why don't you take me to work with you? I could use my sleeping bag and bunk down in your office." YL looked up, his eyes filled with hope.

His father blew on his steamy coffee, then took a sip. "Well, the only helpful thing about all of this is that it won't start this week." He stirred the coffee with a plastic stick. "What was so bad about your other baby-sitter anyway? I thought you liked her. Miss McPurtle believed you were the cutest thing since sliced bread, at least until you pulled that dirty trick on her and hid her false teeth."

YL put down his hot dog. "I didn't *hide* her false teeth, Dad. I just put them where I wouldn't have to look at them."

"Hmmm," Dwayne Truax answered with a frown.

"Dad. She left her teeth in a drinking glass one time in the sink. I went into the kitchen late at night to get a glass of water. Geez louise, there were her uppers and lowers in the glass. They nearly scared me to death."

YL's father smiled. "Remember all the sweaters she crocheted for you?"

"How could I forget?" YL answered. "She only crocheted in pink or lavender."

His father laughed. He looked at the check the waitress left and took money from his wallet. "Well, I'm sure that there's only one Miss McPurtle in the world, and she's still living in Cheyenne."

"I hope so," YL said. He wiped his mouth with a small white paper napkin. "With my luck, she's probably got a twin sister right in Whispering Springs."

"I doubt it," his father replied. "Come on, we can get over to the mall and pick up what you need for tomorrow, if we don't lallygag."

Riding along the highway, YL and his father sat in silence. When the car pulled up to a stop at a red traffic light, YL looked through the windshield into the sky.

"That's another one," YL said suddenly.

"Another what?" his father replied, looking over the steering wheel into the night sky.

"That," YL answered, pointing to the traffic light hanging from the middle of the intersection high above them. "Yellow Light," YL said. "One of the kids at school even guessed that my name was Yellow Light."

"Maybe you ought to just tell them what it stands for," his father offered.

"Wild horses couldn't drag it out of me," YL stated.

CHAPTER SEVEN

Fat Chance!

Around eight-thirty that same night, Sophie Spagnolo tiptoed into the office of the Crescent Moon Motel and picked up the telephone. She dialed a long-distance number with a 302 area code.

Riiiiiiiing. Riiiiiiiiing. Silence.

Riiiiiiiing. Riiiiiiiiing. Silence.

"Hello?" It was Tobias, Fiddle's little brother.

"Hello, is Fiddle home?"

"Who's calling?" Sophie could hear Fiddle laughing in the background.

"Hi, Tobias, it's me, Sophie."

"Oh, hi."

Sophie heard a muffled sound.

"Hey, Fiddle, it's Sophie."

There was a long silence.

Finally, Sophie heard Tobias say, "Fiddle can't come to the phone right now, could you call her back?"

"What do you mean, she can't talk to me right now?"

"She can't. She has friends over."

"Who?" Sophie asked.

"Marla and Bonnie."

"Marla and Bonnie!" Sophie repeated. Fiddle has always hated Marla Gerstwick and Bonnie Sabre, Sophie thought to herself.

"Right," Tobias answered. "Should I tell Fiddle you're going to call back?"

"No, that's okay," Sophie replied. "Thanks, Tobias."

There was a click at the other end.

Sophie put the office phone back into its cradle.

Later, seated at the kitchen table with her father and Lana, Sophie rehearsed her plan. Out the squeaky side door, careful not to let it bang. Crouch low and run alongside the low bushes by the driveway. Check for cars. Dash across the highway. Drop in the letter. Then run like crazy all the way back the length of the hedge to the side door.

"Sophie?" her father said, interrupting her thoughts.

She nearly jumped out of her skin. She and Lana and her father were playing Monopoly at the dining room table. Mr. Spagnolo was helping Lana count her money so that she could buy Indiana Avenue.

"Yes, Dad."

"Why do I have the feeling you're not with us on the planet Earth tonight?"

"Sorry, Dad," she said. She rolled the dice, landed

on a Community Chest and drew a Go to Jail card. "Just my luck," she sighed.

Her father checked his watch. "You're off the hook, it's time for bed, anyway."

Sophie looked out the window as she folded up the game board. Rain misted across the lawn.

"The fog's as thick as buttermilk tonight," he commented, standing beside Sophie and gazing through the windowpanes. "If this weather keeps up, you won't be able to see your hand in front of your face. Mom said she'd be late tonight." He anxiously looked at his watch again.

Sophie sighed with relief. Maybe the fog would be so thick that no one could see anything.

Sophie listened for her father's voice saying good night to Lana. The minute she heard the door to her sister's room close, Sophie tiptoed down the hallway. Her bathrobe fell into a heap beside the door. Wearing only her undies, Sophie stepped onto the porch and started down the steps. Damp, cold air raised goose bumps on her arms and legs. She shivered. Halfway along the hedgerow, she slipped on the wet grass and landed with a thud on her bottom. She sat perfectly still. A car crept along in the fog, its headlight beams sweeping the bushes beside her.

"Go on three," she coached herself. "One. Two. Three." She stood up, ran across the highway, and grabbed the handle on the big blue mailbox. She pulled. She tugged. "Oh, come on," Sophie said aloud.

Stuck! The swinging door to the mailbox was stuck!

Sophie looked from side to side. In the dense fog, she could hear a car's engine coming along the highway.

"Open up, open up," Sophie ordered. She yanked on the handle with all her strength. Magically, the lid gave way. Sophie tossed the envelope into the box's yawning black hole and turned to run across the highway, but a car's fuzzy headlights were already in sight. She crouched beside the mailbox and waited for the car to pass. A red turn signal flashed eerily in the blanket of fog, and Sophie watched in horror as her mother's car pulled into the motel driveway. Her mother got out, rattled the car keys in her hand the way she always did, and walked inside the office.

"Holy cow! Now what?" Sophie asked, her breath making wispy, white clouds. The hairs on her arms and legs stood straight up. Her teeth began to chatter.

A semitrailer rumbled past. As soon as the light in the motel office went out, Sophie made a dash for the bushes. She ran the length of the hedge. She reached for the door handle only to hear her father's voice. "I'll be right there, dear," he called from inside the motel to Sophie's mother. "I just have to lock this side door."

Sophie was sure her heart stopped beating right at that very moment. Then she heard a frightening sound. The lock on the side door clicked and was followed by the unmistakable sound of the chain sliding across the security guard.

"Oh, no. *What* am I going to do?" she whispered.

She ran around to the back of the house. One of the basement windows was open a crack. She pushed the frame with her sneakered foot. The hinges creaked and groaned.

Wet, icy evergreen branches brushed along Sophie's back and legs as she sank to her hands and knees and slid, feet first, through the window. She landed with a thud on a pile of boxes and toppled onto her side. Still catching her breath, she pushed the window closed and groped her way toward the stairs. In the inky blackness, spiderwebs whipped across her face and shoulders.

Every single basement step groaned under her weight. Oh, please, Sophie begged, no noise! All I want to do is make it upstairs without being discovered. The door creaked open to the orange light of the Crescent Moon Motel sign. Sophie retrieved her bathrobe in the half-light of the hallway.

"Sophie," her mother called out.

Sophie jumped. She jammed her other arm into the sleeve of her robe.

"Honey, are you having trouble getting to sleep?"

"Yes, Mom," Sophie answered, thankful that she didn't have to completely lie.

Her mother put her arm around her. "Let's get you back to bed. You're cold as a stone."

Sophie leaned into her mother's shoulder. She climbed into bed wearing her bathrobe.

"Sorry you can't sleep. Were you thinking about school?" her mother asked.

"A little," Sophie said.

"Well, I can sympathize with you about how hard it is to start a new school," Mrs. Spagnolo said. "I realize you've heard this story a dozen times before, but *I* went to four different elementary schools by the time I was your age."

"I know, Mom."

"It's going to take some time, Sophie, that's all there is to it."

"If you say so, Mom."

"You'll make new friends."

"I know, Mom."

Mrs. Spagnolo leaned over and kissed Sophie.

"Trust me, you'll have people lining up to be your friend."

"Okay, Mom."

"Good night, sweetie."

"Good night, Mom."

Sophie heard the bathroom light click on and the door close.

"Lining up to be my friend?" Sophie questioned into the darkness. "Fat chance!"

CHAPTER EIGHT

Eyeball Business

"**W**hat's going on here?" Mrs. TenBroeck asked, walking toward Harper's desk where a cluster of children had congregated. All of them immediately put their hands behind their backs. Tennie stopped beside Charles Whiteside's desk, putting her hands on her hips. "What are you doing, Mr. Whiteside?" she asked, although her question was directed toward the entire crowd of students.

"Nothing, Mrs. TenBroeck," a chorus of voices answered.

"Then why are your hands behind your backs?"

Mrs. TenBroeck surveyed the booklets and papers on Harper's desk. "What's all this?"

Harper handed her teacher a small red booklet. Mrs. TenBroeck slipped her glasses onto the end of her nose.

"*Palm and Fingerprint Reading Made Easy,*" she mumbled.

"We were looking at fingerprints," Harper explained, "trying to tell who's got a peacock's eye or a tented arch."

"Where'd you get this?"

"It's mine. I brought it from home."

"Oh, I see. Is palm reading one of your talents, Miss Stritch?"

Harper nodded. "I'm trying to learn."

Mrs. TenBroeck looked at Harper over her reading glasses.

"Let me see your fingers," the teacher asked, holding Harper's hand, scrutinizing the fingertips.

"All of you," Mrs. TenBroeck ordered, turning around and waving her hand, "palms up!"

Twenty-one pairs of hands with forty-two black thumbs were held in the air.

Mrs. TenBroeck ordered everyone in the class to take out a piece of paper.

"Tented arches," she muttered, looking at her own thumb, moving her bifocals back and forth, holding her thumb closer, then farther away. She jammed her thumb onto Harper's stamp pad and pressed an image onto a small slip of paper. "What's it look like to you?" she asked.

Harper flipped through the pages of the small guidebook.

"Whorls," she advised.

"Whorls?" Mrs. TenBroeck replied. "Harold Pon," she commanded, "come up here and put these new vocabulary words on the board. Tented arches. Peacock's eyes. And don't forget the possessive apostrophe s on peacock's eyes." She turned toward Harold at the chalkboard. "That's whorls with a *wh*, Harold. Now tell me again, Harper, what does it mean to have whorls?"

"Whorls on a few of the fingers mean that instead of daydreaming about things you want to do, you must do them."

"Well, I'll be," Mrs. TenBroeck admitted. She continued studying her thumb. She took off her glasses and looked up. "All those in favor of redefining the learning objective of language arts class today, say 'aye.' "

"Aye!"

"Then tented arches, it is," Mrs. TenBroeck proclaimed. She crumpled the paper with her fingerprint on it and tossed it in the wastebasket. "Can't let the FBI get ahold of that!" she said with a laugh.

Everyone made sets of fingerprints as Mrs. TenBroeck's black and blue stamp pads were passed around. Together, Mrs. TenBroeck and Harper talked the class through the descriptions of tented arches, loops, peacock's eyes, and whorls.

Sophie's tented arches meant she had stick-to-it-iveness. YL's loops were a sign of good-natured friendliness, and Harper already knew that the peacock's eye on her pinkies predicted she was a born writer.

Unannounced, Mr. Workel stepped into Room 17. He held his hands behind his back and cleared his throat. There was such a humming and buzzing of students working on their creative writing that at first no one heard him. Mrs. TenBroeck was talking with Carnell Witherspoon and standing beside Sunday Margolis's desk. The students exchanged papers, reading what they had written about the fingerprints they had deciphered. Mr. Workel cleared his throat a second time. Everyone looked up. The room immediately fell silent.

"And just exactly what enthralling educational 'experience' are we providing the children with today, Mrs. TenBroeck? If I asked to see your plan book, would this charming lesson be in there?"

Every child in Room 17 watched as Mrs. TenBroeck turned pale as a ghost.

Harper looked at her teacher, then stood up and walked past her to Mr. Workel.

"Come on over here, sir," she said, taking the principal by the hand and leading him to the nearest stamp pad which was on Loren Ostergaard's desk. "Mr. Workel," Harper asked with all sincerity, taking a sturdy grip on his thumb and placing it firmly on the sticky, black ink pad, "have you ever been fingerprinted?" Everyone heard Mr. Workel gasp when he saw the smeary mess on his thumb. "Absolutely not," he said emphatically.

Harper held Mr. Workel's thumb dangerously near his white shirt. "Well, then, Mr. Workel, how would you know whether you have peacock's eyes or tented arches?"

*   *   *

The pungent smells of spaghetti sauce and steamed corn filled the cafeteria. YL, Sophie, and Harper sat together at one of the big foldout tables. Sophie hadn't said one word as the three of them walked through the lunch line.

"Are you sick or something?" Harper quizzed Sophie.

YL looked up, waiting for her answer.

Sophie sighed, then spoke, "No."

"Has your quiet mood got something to do with that club?" Harper asked.

YL turned to her. "What club?"

Harper waved her fork in the air as she spoke. "The Faith, Hope, and Charity Club. The one Melody Briscoe's in."

YL looked confused. "I've never heard of it. Does it have to do with something at school?"

"Nope," Harper answered. "It's just a bunch of girls that think they have to have a club to belong to. And Sophie here is thinking of joining."

YL raised his eyebrows. "Oh," he replied, still looking puzzled. "Can boys belong?"

"Nope," Harper said, using her fork to point at Sophie, "and that's another strike against it in my book."

YL shook his head, turning to Sophie. "How come you want to belong to a club?"

She shrugged.

Harper leaned across the table. "Now listen, Sofe. We could start our own club, just the three of us. You, me, and Yahoo over there," Harper said, looking at YL.

"My name's not Yahoo."

Harper ignored YL's remark. "We could call ourselves the . . . the . . ." she started to say. "We could call ourselves the . . ."

YL helped her out. "Faith, Hope, and . . ." he began, but also became stuck on the last part.

Sophie looked up.

"Faith, Hope, and . . ." YL repeated, his eyebrows wrinkled with concentration.

"I've got it," Harper said, jumping out of her chair and waving her arms in the air. Other students turned to look at her. "The Faith, Hope, and Chicken Feathers Club." Harper sat down.

"Chicken Feathers?" YL asked.

Harper leaned across the table until she was almost nose to nose with Sophie. "That's what we'll call ourselves. We'll start our own club." She smiled a fiendish smile at YL. "Even boys can be in it. The only requirement is that you have to be a new kid in the sixth grade." Harper tapped Sophie's shirt with the fork. "Sofe, you can be the faith, I'll be the hope, and Mr. YL Truax, here, can be the chicken feathers."

"Thanks a heap," YL said. He stood up, grabbing his plastic lunch tray. "You're a certified nut cake if I ever saw one," he told Harper and headed toward the dirty-dish conveyor belt. "Don't hold your breath waiting for me to join," he said over his shoulder.

Sophie almost smiled, but she still didn't say anything. She poked her fork at the spaghetti on her plate and watched a solitary meatball roll around the edge. "Do you want my eyeball?" she offered Harper.

"Eyeball?"

"I mean meatball," Sophie said nervously.

Harper stabbed Sophie's meatball.

"What's up, Sofe? You're a real bag of nerves today," Harper said with her mouth full. "Are you going to tell me or what?" When Sophie didn't answer, Harper only shook her head.

Sophie remained silent, even as the two girls walked outside for recess.

"I forgot something," Sophie told Harper by the stairs. "You go without me."

Harper frowned but went on, alone.

Sophie thought her stomach had crept into her throat as she walked back to Room 17. Goose bumps popped up on her arms, although the radiators clanked and hissed heat. Her fingers felt slippery and clammy as she opened Steve Coffinburger's desk. The dark green velvet box Melo described lay half hidden under a layer of crumpled math and social studies papers.

Sophie pulled on the lid of the box, trying to get it open. "Jammed," she mumbled. "Oh, rats!" She tugged. The lid clicked open. "Oh, my," she whispered. An unblinking, green-irised eyeball stared up at her.

Harper appeared at the door. "Sofe! What are you doing?"

Sophie jumped. Her fingers suddenly felt like they were coated with butter. The velvet case slipped from her grasp, tumbling to the floor.

The two girls watched as Steve's spare eyeball slipped

out of the case and clunked onto the floor, and like a giant marble, rolled away from them.

"Quick!" Harper ordered.

She and Sophie scrambled to their hands and knees, the eyeball just out of reach.

"Oh, no," Sophie gasped as the eyeball rolled across a cold-air grate, dropped through an opening and landed with a resounding clunk.

The two girls peered into the gray metallic box of ductwork.

Harper tugged at the grate, lifting it off and setting it aside. She pushed up her sleeve.

"What are you doing?" Sophie asked.

"Going after it, what else?"

Sophie felt tears well up. "I hope it didn't break."

"I'm sure it didn't," Harper's voice echoed. "Glass eyeballs don't break. I think I can see it." Both girls lay on their stomachs, legs splayed, heads and shoulders side by side.

"What are we going to do?" Sophie asked.

Harper looked at Sophie. "I'm going eyeball fishing, but the real question is, what are *you* going to do?"

Sophie's eyes began to tear up again.

"What I ought to do, Sofe, is let you roast, if you ask me," Harper said, shaking her head. "This eyeball business has something to do with that dumb club, doesn't it?"

Sophie looked away. "Yes," she admitted softly.

Harper stretched her arm into the dark cavity. "Oh, yuck," she muttered, "spiderwebs." Her fingers emerged from the darkness, covered with the fuzz of white, thready spiderweb strands. "We're going to need something longer." She looked around. "Where's Mrs. TenBroeck's spear, I mean pointer?"

Sophie took it from the chalkboard tray and handed it to Harper who crawled under Christa Billetts' desk and pulled off two old pieces of pink chewing gum that were stuck to the bottom. She popped the gum into her mouth and gave a few quick chews.

"Oh, yuck," Sophie gagged.

"Well," Harper said, taking the gum from her mouth, "it's got to be sticky. That's a heavy eyeball down there." She took the gum and stuck it to the end of the pointer, then poked the pointer into the duct-work. "Got it," she said, carefully lifting the pointer hand over hand so she wouldn't jar the precariously attached eyeball. Harper held the glass eye in her hand. "Wow, it's not what I thought it would look like at all." She handed it to Sophie. The two stared at their prize. "You want my opinion?"

Sophie looked up. She wasn't sure whether to answer yes or no.

"If I were you, I'd just put it back in Steve's desk and forget the whole dumb thing."

"But . . ."

Harper refitted the grate, stood up, and brushed off her clothes. "I'd tell those girls in the Faith, Hope, and Charity Club that if they want to see Steve Coffinburger's glass eye bad enough, they can steal it for themselves."

"But then I'll never get in the club."

"True, but are you sure you want to be in their club? You could have me and YL in the Faith, Hope, and Chicken Feathers Club. What more could you ask for?"

Harper pulled the wad of gum off the pointer and flicked it into the wastebasket. Sophie returned the pointer to the chalk tray. "But Melody wanted me to take it because she said all the girls in the club wanted to see it."

"Well, we're girls, and we've seen it now, haven't we?" Harper held the box open. Sophie placed the eyeball into the small, nested spot inside. Harper held the open box up to the light coming in through the window. "Why don't you tell Melo and Suki that Steve's glass eyeball has sparkles through the green part and little tiny red bloodshot lines in the white part. Then tell them that if they've got the guts to steal an eyeball for themselves, you'd consider asking them to join *our* club. If you ask me, I think they're the ones that are a bunch of gutless wonders." Footsteps sounded on the stairs. "Here," Harper said, shoving the box into Sophie's hands like a hot potato, "you take this. I don't want a noose around my neck. I'm no eyeball thief."

Harper dashed out of the room in the direction of the stairs.

The click, click, click of Mrs. TenBroeck's high heels grew louder. Sophie had to make her decision quickly. The first thing she did was close the box, thankful the eyeball could no longer stare at her.

Mrs. TenBroeck walked between the rows of desks. "Take this paper home over the weekend and ask your parents to help you fill it in. We're going to do some work with family history. Ask your parents if they can help you write down the names on your family tree. Try to include as many relatives as you can, things like your grandparents' names. Cousins. Where you were born, where your parents were born. Do you understand?"

Everyone nodded.

"Then once you've got all of that written down, we'll start working with them next week. Turn up all the family skeletons you can. Ask about everyone. All the horse thieves and scalawags in your distinguished family lineage," Mrs. TenBroeck said, walking past Bobby Ray McKinnon. "For instance, Mr. McKinnon, someone in your family might have been a distinguished general in the Civil War."

"Who, me, Mrs. TenBroeck?" he asked, rubbing his hand over his crew cut. "Naw, not in my family, but I have an Uncle Willie who's pretty famous. He's doing time in prison for forgery."

Mrs. TenBroeck smiled. "Fame comes in lots of different varieties, Mr. McKinnon," she admitted, patting Bobby Ray on the back. "A long time ago, I had an Aunt Fiona who won the Irish Sweepstakes." Mrs.

TenBroeck licked her thumb and passed out another form. "Well, ladies and germs, see what you can unearth. We'll hang the family time lines all along the wall here," she said, pointing to the side bulletin board, "Kind of our own little Whispering Springs Rogues' Gallery." She looked up at the big clock on the side wall.

"Next week we'll form work groups and start building dioramas of Inuit villages." She ruffled Charles Whiteside's hair as she walked past him.

Crosby's hand shot up. "What's a diarrhea, Mrs. TenBroeck?"

She laughed. "It's not di-ar-rhea, Crosby. It's di-o-rama."

"Oh," he answered, still not understanding.

"It's like a little scene," Mrs. TenBroeck explained. "You can make an Inuit scene out of whatever you can find and secure it on big pieces of cardboard." She looked at the clock again. "Let's get ready so we can go home, shall we? Quietly, please, my little polar bears." She walked to the front of the room and took a stack of papers off the top of her desk. The clock buzzed.

"Be sure to have these signed by your 'significant' parent," Mrs. TenBroeck said, handing slips to each student as they filed out of the room for the day.

"What are they for?" Rayna Abrams asked.

"It's not a good idea to end your sentences with a preposition," Mrs. TenBroeck reminded. "I'll let it slip this one time, Rayna, and answer your question. The school board has graciously seen the light and earmarked some budget money for travel, and I intend to spend every penny and nickel of it before they change their minds. We're taking a field trip in two weeks, and I'll need the slips signed, sealed, and delivered to me next week."

"Where are we going?" Sunday Margolis asked.

Mrs. TenBroeck licked her thumb and peeled another form off the stack. "Washington, D.C.," she replied.

"Wow," Bobby Ray said. "That's farther away than my cousin's house in Cumberland, in Maryland, isn't it?"

"I thought your cousin was in prison," Mrs. Ten-Broeck answered.

"Nope," Bobby Ray answered matter-of-factly, "that's my uncle."

"Remember, my little rutabagas," Mrs. TenBroeck added, "I need these signed, sealed, and delivered back to me *or* you don't go on the trip."

Sophie left the room, looking both ways along the back corridor, and started down the stairs. Melo and Suki stepped out of the stairwell, blocking her path.

"Well, Sofa, will I get the envelope in the mail?" Melo asked.

"Yes," Sophie answered.

"Good. Very good. So where's Steve's glass eye?" Suki asked.

"Yeah, where's the eyeball?" Melo repeated.

Sophie looked at both of them and felt her knees wobble. "In his desk," she answered.

Melo walked up a step and looked down the corridor, checking for teachers.

"I don't have it," Sophie explained.

"What do you mean, you don't have it?" Suki said.

"I mean, I left it in Steve's desk."

"Why didn't you take it?" Melody asked.

Sophie tried to remember what Harper had said to say. "I did take it. I saw it all right, saw it just fine. It's really neat. It has these little green sparkly things around the center part, and it even has fake bloodshot lines. It's smooth, too. Almost slippery. It's in this dark green velvet box that has a satin lining."

Melo interrupted. "What a stupe. You were supposed to *take* it and *give* it to us. So *we* could see it," she said, pointing to herself.

Sophie thought for a second about what she ought to say next. She tried hard to get the words right, the words Harper had said. "Well, if you have the guts to steal his eyeball, then you can see for yourselves just how neat it is."

Suki stepped closer to Sophie. "Hey, don't you talk to us like that. Remember, Sofa, we're the ones who sent *you* on a mission." Suki sneered at Sophie. "This is going to cost you, Spagnolo. What makes you think you can give us some rip-snot answer like that?"

Melo put her face up to Sophie's. "You can't go against the club like that, Sofa. Not if you want to be one of us."

Sophie noticed Melo's white-blond eyelashes for the very first time.

"You and Suki said that all I had to do was take his eyeball," Sophie insisted. "You didn't say specifically what I was supposed to do with it. So I took it and looked at it like you said."

Suki crossed her arms and stepped beside Melo. "Listen to her. Now she sounds like a lawyer."

"You're not going to get away with this," Melo said.

"I'm not so sure you deserve to be in the club, anyway," Suki added.

Melo and Suki turned and began walking away from Sophie. "Have a good time at dance class, Sophie, the Sofa, Spagnolo," Melo said.

Sophie opened her mouth to say that she didn't care about their stupid old club, that they could keep their dorky missions. But somehow, the strength to form this new string of words escaped her. She sank down and sat on the step, wondering how her legs would ever have the power to carry her all the way to Miss Natalie's.

"Hey, Sofe, wait up! You look as pale as a ghost," Harper yelled as she ran along the sidewalk to catch up with her friend. She grabbed Sophie's arm. "Is it the club?"

Sophie kept walking but didn't answer.

Harper stayed by her side until they reached the entrance to Miss Natalie's. "Want some company?" Harper asked. "I could always sit and watch along with the mothers and baby-sitters and little brothers. I could pretend I'm your sister or something."

Sophie still didn't answer. Harper followed her friend through the back door. The two walked down the steps to the dressing room.

Harper waited while Sophie changed into her dance tights and leotard.

"I always wanted to take dance lessons," Harper said. "My mom's promised me I could someday."

"I don't feel so good," Sophie said, "I have a wicked stomachache."

"Do you have to go to dance class?" Harper asked.

"My mom'll kill me if I don't," Sophie answered.

The two walked down a long corridor, approaching the studio area where the sound of piano music grew louder. Standing outside the door marked REST ROOM, they heard a noise. *Kaa-blooie! Bang! Crash!*

The girls turned. *Kerplunk! Wham!* Then they heard the sound of glass shattering. A voice mumbled, "Geez louise."

"What's going on?" Harper asked.

"Hey in there?" Sophie said, walking up to the door. No answer.

The girls looked at each other. Harper opened the door, and they took a step into the rest room.

Both girls gasped, then put their hands over their mouths to stop giggling.

Before them stood a dancer. Not your ordinary ballet student, but a dancer clad in a pair of dark-purple tights, black ballet slippers, and white T-shirt.

Sophie and Harper held their breath.

The dancer was YL.

CHAPTER NINE

And One, and Two, and Three

"**D**on't say anything," YL ordered. "Don't you dare tell a soul."

Sophie grabbed Harper's arm.

"We won't have to," she told YL. "The minute you walk out on that dance floor, everyone in Whispering Springs is going to know you're in Miss Natalie's dance class."

He held his arms out to show his costume. "This whole thing was my dad's idea." YL looked miserable. "Now I'm a koinkydink, nerd ballet dancer."

Harper motioned for YL to come out of the dressing room. "Don't worry, YL, it's not the end of the world."

"Right," he said forlornly, "you're not the one prancing out there in a pair of eggplant tights. The store was out of black ones."

"How come you're taking dance lessons? Does your dad want you to be a dancer?" Harper asked.

"Well, not exactly. It's a deal we made. See, I told my dad that I wanted to try out for the football team next year, but he said I couldn't unless I took dance lessons first. But I kept telling him that I didn't think any other guys went to Miss Natalie's, and he said, 'So what?' "

"I don't get it," Sophie questioned, "what's football got to do with ballet?"

YL looked thoroughly exasperated. "My dad has this theory that if I'm going to be a great football player, I ought to train as a ballet dancer, like Joe Namath did. That way, I can learn how to move better on a football field."

Miss Natalie's voice drifted in from the other room. "And one, and two, and three, and four."

"Well, Joe, you're about to find out," Harper snickered. "All you have to do is pirouette onto the dance floor." She giggled, holding open the door.

Sophie stepped forward. "Take one giant leap, YL. Look at me. Sophie, the Sofa, the human whale, in a leotard." She held up her arm in a sweeping motion. "I've managed to go to Miss Natalie's. I'm absolute living proof that a human being can withstand the jeers and sneers of ballet."

YL did not look convinced.

Miss Natalie's voice droned, "Second position. Ready. And one, and two, and three, and four," as her yardstick with Faust's Hardware and Supply written along the flat front tapped the floor.

"Yosemite," Harper said suddenly.

"What?" YL asked.

"Yosemite. I bet your name's Yosemite Lionel Truax," she replied.

"Come on, Sophie," YL said, "let's bite the bullet and go out there. I'd rather do anything than listen to Harper, here, try and guess my name. Like I told you, Harp, it's going to be a long cold day in July before you even come close."

Harper watched in amazement as YL leaped into the hallway and walked onto the dance floor. Miss Natalie stopped counting.

"And who do we have here?" she asked, the yardstick caught in midair.

YL flinched.

"Ah, yes, you must be the Truax boy. I spoke with your father about lessons, didn't I? Take your position, Mr. Future Football Hero," she ordered. "As for you, Miss Spagnolo, you're *late* again!" Suki Lufflin smirked. Headache lines furrowed Miss Natalie's forehead. Sophie held back a smile, knowing the class would probably be dismissed early, which meant that she and YL could go up to Harper's apartment for a while.

Miss Natalie turned and nodded to a birdlike, gray-haired woman at the piano. "Third position, everyone." Miss Natalie walked to the center of the room and tapped her yardstick on the floor. The piano accompaniment began. "Ready? And one, and two, and three, and four."

"My mom's at practice until nine-thirty," Harper told YL and Sophie as they came into the apartment.

Jupiter curled around YL's legs. He reached down to pick her up. She rolled over in his arms as if asking him to scratch her tummy.

"I never saw so many plants," YL said, eyeing the pots of lush green leaves cascading along every window casing and trailing from dark orange pots on windowsills. YL sat on the sofa. Jupiter climbed onto his shoulders, purring directly into his ear. "It's almost like this cat can talk," he commented.

"My mom's crazy about plants," Harper said. "She even talks to her African violets."

"African violets?" YL asked. "I think my mom has some of those. Do they have little flowers?" Jupiter draped herself around YL's shoulders like a scarf and licked him on the ear. "Hey, that tickles," he said, patting her on the head.

Harper pointed to a row of dark green plants with small, vivid purple flowers lining the windowsill above the kitchen sink. "Mom says that her conversations with them are why they have so many flowers." Harper rolled her eyes. "Sometimes my mom is just too weird for words."

Sophie stood by the kitchen table and picked up a small, white, rectangular sugar cube. "What are these for?" she asked Harper.

"Our diorama," Harper answered. She took several cubes and stacked them one on top of the other. She uncapped a bottle of Elmer's Glue-All. "I was trying an experiment . . ."

"Oh, wow, look at this," Sophie said, pulling out a

chair and sitting down. She made a semicircle of sugar cubes. "They're perfect for making an igloo. They look like the right shape, but we need to cut some of them in half."

"Break them with your teeth," Harper advised, "like this." She placed a cube between her back teeth and bit down. The cube neatly halved itself. The two girls began gluing and arranging the cubes. "What do you think? Does it look like an igloo?" Harper asked YL, who was still wearing Jupiter on his shoulders.

YL dumped the cat onto the couch, stood up, and walked over to the table. He looked at the igloo from several different angles. "If I squint long enough, it might."

"Maybe we could use marshmallows," Sophie suggested.

"Yeah, maybe marshmallows would make the walls look less pointy," YL added.

A car honked outside.

Sophie looked toward the window. She stood up. "It's Evan," she explained. "And I'd better hustle my bustle. Last time, he hollered at me, big time, for taking so long to come out."

"I'd better get out there, too. My dad gets crabby when I make him wait," YL said.

Harper walked them both to the door and started down the stairs. Jupiter waited at the top of the landing. "What do you want for your birthday present?" Harper asked.

"Oh, that's okay," YL explained, "you don't have to bring a present."

"I bet I can find something between now and Saturday. See you tomorrow at school," Harper said as YL and Sophie disappeared around the corner.

Harper went back to the table and began gluing more sugar cubes onto the base of the original circle. Jupiter jumped up beside her.

"You know, Jupe, we've got this club we're going to have with Sophie and YL and me in it."

The cat blinked as if she understood.

Harper squirted a blob of glue onto another white cube. "We're calling ourselves the Faith, Hope, and Chicken Feathers Club." She squarely placed the cube onto the stack and pushed down until glue oozed along the edges. "You're not a sixth grader, but you're new. Why don't we have you be our mascot?" she asked the cat.

Jupiter purred loudly.

"I'll take that as a yes," Harper said, stroking the cat's arching back. "Want a sugar cube?" She held a piece of sugar for Jupiter to sniff.

Harper tilted her head and looked directly into Jupiter's face. "What do you say, Jupe? Maybe Whispering Springs won't be as lonely as every other town we've lived in now that there's Sophie and YL."

Jupiter rubbed her face against Harper's cheek.

"I'll take that as another yes," she answered, feeling a deep, throaty smile come to her lips, not unlike Jupiter's vibrating purr.

CHAPTER TEN

Punkin Face, Yellow Light, and Nosey Rosey

Only ten people had checked into the motel, and the evening was a slow one. Sophie and her mother sat next to each other on the couch in the office while Mr. Spagnolo made another attempt at fixing the sign outside.

Sophie loved looking at the pictures in her baby book. A favorite was one of Evan, who was six at the time, holding her on his lap in front of the birch tree. Then there was a snapshot of the two of them on their parents' double bed.

"Naked as jaybirds," Sophie's mother said, every time anyone saw the picture. "Just look at those bare bums hanging out like that." Mrs. Spagnolo laughed. Sophie smiled, but her expression quickly changed as her mother turned the page.

"Oh, look," Mrs. Spagnolo commented, "here are the first pictures of you and Fiddle. These were taken the summer we moved into the house on Fifth Avenue in Magnolia."

Sophie's mother paused.

"Has Fiddle written?"

"Nope."

"I heard you talking on the phone the other night. I thought maybe you'd had a chance to talk to her."

"Nope." Sophie thought for a moment about telling her mother what had happened, but decided against it.

"Have you tried to make any new friends here, honey?"

"Sure, Mom," Sophie answered, quickly flipping through the other pictures in the baby book. "Some of them will be at YL's birthday party on the weekend. Harper will be there. I guess you could say that we're friends."

"Sometime, you'll have to ask Harper over here," Mrs. Spagnolo said, standing up. "She could spend the night. You could stay up late. Watch TV. Eat pizza. Do things like that," she added, reaching down to tickle Sophie in the ribs. "By the way, YL's an interesting name for your little boyfriend," she commented.

Sophie made a ghastly face. "Mom, YL's not my boyfriend."

"Oh, okay. I didn't mean it that way. I meant your *male* friend, YL. Is that better?" She stepped behind the desk and straightened the wrinkled register pages.

"He won't tell us what the YL stands for," Sophie said. "Have you got any ideas, Mom?"

Sophie's question hung in the air as Mrs. Spagnolo answered the motel phone. "Crescent Moon Motel," she said efficiently.

"It's for you, sweetie," her mother said, handing her the phone.

When Sophie mouthed the words, "Who is it?" her mother shook her head and held up her hands.

Fiddle, Sophie instantly thought to herself. *It must be Fiddle!*

"Hello?" Sophie asked into the phone.

"Hey, Sofe? Is that you?"

"Yes," she answered, not recognizing the voice.

"Hi, it's me."

Sophie still didn't recognize the voice.

"It's me, Harper, you ditz brain."

Sophie put her hand over the mouthpiece and took a breath.

"Oh, my gosh, Harper. Hi! I didn't recognize your voice at first. How are you? What do you want?"

"Well, I'm calling about YL's birthday party on Saturday. I was wondering if you'd like to go together and get YL a present? I don't have much money. Only three dollars and seventy-three cents. But maybe we could pool what we have and get something pretty decent. What do you think?"

Sophie clamped her hand over the phone again. She hadn't bought YL anything yet for his birthday, and her own resources were a little on the low side after buying the crayons for Lana.

"Sure," Sophie answered, "got any ideas?"

"Well, since he likes baseball, how about getting him a set of baseball cards. Or maybe a hat. I could ask tomorrow what his favorite team is."

"That sounds good," Sophie said. "I think that sounds fine."

"Okay," Harper replied. There was an awkward pause. "I guess that's everything for right now, huh?"

"Yeah," Sophie agreed, "I guess that's everything." There was another empty pause. "Hey, Harp, is your mother home yet?"

"Nope, she won't be home for another hour."

"Oh."

"But Jupiter's here with me."

"Did you cook your own dinner?"

"Yep."

"What'd you have?"

"Macaroni and cheese."

"Again?"

"Yep."

"Did you eat it all?"

"Nope, but Jupiter finished it. She loves macaroni and cheese. She even loves the hot-dog pieces."

The other phone rang at the motel.

"Well, talk to you tomorrow."

"Right. Talk to you tomorrow."

"I have to go now. My mom doesn't want me hogging the motel phone."

"Okay. We can decide on the present tomorrow."

"Great."

"Well, see you tomorrow."

"Okay, see you tomorrow."

There was another staticky pause.

"Hey, Harper, are you still there?"

"Yeah."

"Thanks for calling," Sophie said.

"Hey, anytime, Sofe. Talk to you tomorrow."

"Bye."

"Yeah, bye."

Sophie put down the phone.

"Thanks for calling," she repeated, suddenly realizing how much she meant it.

On her way to the Dumpster with a bag of garbage, Sophie heard her father call out to her from a ladder by the neon sign.

"Hey, punkin face, look over here," he cried. "Are you ready for this?" Sophie smiled and gave him the okay sign. She watched her father connect another light tube, and the sign flickered on.

"That's great, Dad, you're getting closer," Sophie hollered as the words Crescent Moo flashed on and off.

While YL's father was watching a basketball game on TV, YL dialed the phone in the kitchen.

"Hello, Mom? It's me, YL."

"Hi, sweetie, how are you? Wait a minute, honey." YL heard his mother put her hand over the mouthpiece and say something. YL thought he heard a girl's giggling voice.

"Who's there?" he asked when she came back on the line.

"Oh, some friends."

"Who?"

"Oh, it's Phillip. Now don't go getting nosey on me, YL Truax. How are you, sweetie?"

"I'm fine, but I need my birth certificate for a project at school. Do you have a copy you could send me?"

"Sure thing. What kind of project? How's school? Have you made any friends yet? Are you set for your birthday party this weekend?"

"Yep."

"Who did you ask?"

"Every kid in my class."

"Wow, I'm impressed. Your father's going to buy pizza for that many kids?"

"That's what he said."

"Well, good for him."

YL heard his mother put her hand over the phone again and say something.

"Mom?"

"Yes, I'm here, honey. Listen, sweetie, I'm going to call over the weekend. Then you can tell me every little thing about your party. Okay?"

"Okay." There was a moment of silence. Small voices faded in and out, little mystery voices drifting along the phone lines from conversations in Kansas City or Atlanta or Spokane or places even farther away.

"Mom?" YL asked. "You won't forget about the birth certificate, will you?"

"No, sweetie. I can take care of that tomorrow and stick it in the mail to you. You'll have it by Monday or

Tuesday at the latest. Do you want me to write down the names of your grandparents, too?"

"Sure, that would be great."

"Okay, talk to you soon, sweetie. You sleep tight. And when you wake up on your birthday, you'll be a whole year older. Just think, my little baby boy's going to be twelve years old."

"If you say so, Mom," YL answered, shaking his head.

"Talk to you soon. Thanks for calling, honey." He heard his mother's hand go over the phone again. He was positive he heard girls giggling this time.

"Bye, Mom."

"Bye, sweetie. I love you, YL Truax," she said.

"Love you, too, Mom," he repeated. He slowly hung up the phone. *Phillip?* he wondered to himself. *Who was this Phillip guy, anyway?*

During the "Oldies but Goodies Movie Time," Harper sat on the couch with her mother watching television. Seated side by side they laughed at the antics of two slapstick comedians in an old black-and-white movie, *Abbott and Costello Meet the Mummy*. When a commercial came on, Harper got up to get some more cheddar cheese popcorn. Without looking at her mother, she asked, "Hey, Mom, do you know where my birth certificate or baby book are? I need them for school."

The color drained from Caroline Stritch's face.

"You didn't need your birth certificate to get into school. Why on earth would you want it now?" Her voice was unusually strained.

"We have to make a family tree for school," Harper explained, returning with a bowl full of yellow-orange popcorn.

"Oh, Harper, there's probably a birth certificate around here somewhere, but I don't have the vaguest notion where it is. You know, we've moved so many times that I bet it was lost years ago."

"Could you look for it?"

"Now? No, not now, but if I have time tomorrow, I will. Maybe after I get home from practice. Promise me you won't go tearing through everything while I'm gone," she warned. "I don't want this whole place turned upside down."

Abbott and Costello returned to the screen.

Harper plopped down on the sofa and held out the bowl of popcorn for her mother, who took a handful. Harper stared at the TV. "One of the kids at school asked me about my dad," Harper said. Credits for the movie scrolled across the screen. "I must be the only kid in the class who doesn't have a dad."

Harper's mother took another handful of popcorn.

"All I want to do is know more about him," Harper said.

"You're turning into a Nosey Rosey," Caroline Stritch commented. She got up and set the popcorn bowl on the sink. "Time for bed," she said, looking at her watch.

Harper watched the screen, but asked, "Are you sure my baby book isn't somewhere? I'm going to be the only kid in class with no time line. I'm the only kid in the class with no father."

"I guarantee you, Harper, you had a father once. That's what really counts," her mother reminded her.

CHAPTER ELEVEN

Peri winkle

Friday afternoon in Room 17, no one seemed to want to do any work. After the last recess, Mrs. Ten-Broeck started another chapter from *Children of the Northern Lights*. This time, she sat on the opposite corner of her desk.

> Chapter Three: Grandmother's gentle voice and the slight touch of Steps Softly's hand on my cheek woke me.
>
> "You tended the lamp well," Grandmother praised, motioning toward the flame under the stone pot.
>
> I was relieved to see the bright flame still burning. I smiled, stretched, and sat up. "Today, I must find food for us."
>
> While I dressed, Grandmother gnawed on the edges of my kamiks, working out the stiffness. Steps Softly laughed as I poked my head in and out of the hood of my caribou jacket, playing peekaboo with her. I pulled on hareskin stockings, then my boots. I stuffed mit-

tens, extra fishing line, and snow goggles into the pockets of my pants and crawled out of the warmth of our igloo.

The night before, with the storm whipping around our heads, I had helped Father make a shelter for the pups. I licked the flat edge of my walrus ivory knife to glaze a cutting edge. I sliced open a small doorway for them. Apoppa and Tiintuk leaped out, greeting me with yaps and nips at the toes of my boots.

I picked them up, and they squirmed and wriggled in my arms. Apoppa chewed on my chin while Tiin-tuk pinched my fingers with sharp baby teeth. The happiness on my face came from my heart. I was truly grateful Father had given me these pups, for very few dogs were ever given to girls.

Mrs. TenBroeck looked up. Harper smiled. Melody glared. Mrs. TenBroeck continued.

I shooed Tiintuk into the igloo to give Steps Softly a playmate for the day. I tucked Apoppa into my hood the way Mother tucked Steps Softly into her amauk. I picked up Father's hunting spear and held out my hand to Grandmother.

She quickly slipped off my mitten and gently bit my finger. "For good luck," she said, smiling.

I stepped out of our igloo, strapped on the carved wooden snow goggles, and set off in the direction of the ice floes where I hoped Apoppa and I might find many plump fish.

If only, I thought. If only I could catch something.

Father would wear a proud face. Oh, the important story he would have to tell everyone he met for many evenings by the firelight. And more than giving Father a good story to tell, the fish would mean the promise of food for several days.

"Fish, Apoppa," I whispered to the puppy nestled in my hood. "Let us go hunting this morning for fish. With Grandmother's luck, we will find many."

Mrs. TenBroeck looked up at the clock and closed the book, setting it on the desk.

"All right, my little sled dogs. Homework for the weekend is the following." She began writing a list of things to do on the board. "Put the finishing touches on your family histories. And! Remember! Remember! Remember those permission slips for the field trip!" Mrs. TenBroeck turned around to write more words on the board.

Harper slipped Bobby Ray a note for Sophie.

What baseball team? Cards? or Hat?

Sophie nodded, then scribbled *Detroit Tigers . . . Hat,* and stuck the note across the aisle for Bobby Ray to return to Harper, only to find Mrs. TenBroeck standing squarely beside Bobby Ray's desk.

"I just love intercepting notes," Mrs. TenBroeck said, holding out her hand. Sophie felt her cheeks flush to bright red as her teacher took the note and opened it. Mrs. TenBroeck didn't look up as she spoke, but instead, walked to the front of the room. "And the Room Seventeen rule about writing notes, Emily Willcox?"

"You said," Emily recited, looking sympathetically at Sophie, "all notes are *fair game*."

Mrs. TenBroeck held up the note, looking at Sophie. "Shall I read this little . . . exchange between you and Miss Stritch?"

"I wish you wouldn't," Sophie mumbled.

"Pardon me, Miss Spagnolo. I don't believe I heard you all the way up here."

"She says she wishes you wouldn't," Harper repeated.

Mrs. TenBroeck took off her glasses. "Thank you, Miss Stritch, but Sophie doesn't appear to have lost her voice."

Everyone stared at the clock as the buzzer to go home began to sound.

"Saved by the bell," Mrs. TenBroeck said. She let the note drop to her desk.

Sophie gave a sigh of relief.

Mrs. TenBroeck walked over to the door. "Quietly, please. Line up for first bus. Miss Spagnolo, you're not off the hook just yet. I'd like to have a word with you."

The doors of #128 opened abruptly, and Mr. Duke removed his cap and scratched his head. Chattering students filed onto the bus. The second Sophie stood on the bottom step, she remembered. Lana's birthday present. The crayons. Sophie immediately turned pale.

"What's the matter, Sophie?" Mr. Duke asked.

"Oh, Mr. Duke, I left something in my desk for my

sister's birthday party on Sunday. Do I have time to go back and get it?"

Mr. Duke frowned and looked into the big mirror above the front window.

"If you hurry. I'll just pull up at the end of this driveway," he explained. "I'll wait for you there. Where's Lana, anyway?"

"At a Blue Bird Girls meeting," Sophie answered, already running toward the building. "I'll hurry," she shouted. She took the stairs two at a time. Swung into the room. Slid to a stop by her desk. Pulled the box of crayons from underneath a pile of books. And headed out the door. She ran toward the bus and leaped onto the bottom step.

"Not bad," Mr. Duke commented, looking at his watch. "One minute and forty-five seconds." Sophie smiled. She was too winded to talk. She plopped into the first seat behind Mr. Duke.

In between breaths, she said, "Thanks, Mr. Duke." She steadied her backpack on the floor between her feet. "You really saved my life."

The bus rumbled out of the school parking lot. Stopping. Starting up. Lights flashing. Stopping. Starting up. Children spilling out. Past the gas station. Past the drilling company. Past the turn for the cemetery. Sophie was the only person left on the bus.

"So tell me, Sophie," Mr. Duke started to say, smiling, "what do you do if your big toe falls off?"

Sophie laughed. "I don't know, Mr. Duke. What do you do if your big toe falls off?"

"You call a tow truck," he said, looking into the mirror and waiting for her response.

Sophie smiled. "I like that one. A tow truck," she repeated. She still held the box of crayons in her hand. Her heart had finally stopped pounding.

The bus slowed down as it approached the motel. Mr. Duke flicked the switch for the caution lights. Then the red lights. He cranked the STOP sign into position. No cars were coming in front of or behind the bus.

"So that's Lana's birthday present, huh?" he asked, eyeing the box of crayons.

"Yep, she loves to color. I already bought a coloring book for her, but she got in my dresser drawer and found it, so I bought these at school and hid them in my desk."

"There's something nice about a brand-new, unused box of crayons," he admitted.

"I know what you mean," Sophie replied. "I think they look so pretty before they get all chewed up. This set has three new colors. Do you want to see them?"

Mr. Duke checked for traffic. "Sure." Not a car was in sight. He held out his hand for the rubber bands. "Why not?"

Sophie removed the elastic bands and looped them on Mr. Duke's thumbs.

"My favorite color is . . ." she began to say, lifting off the lid. "Oh, no," she cried out, her hand suddenly feeling cold and frozen. She stared at the contents of the box. Mr. Duke stared, too.

"Well, for heaven's sake, Sophie," Mr. Duke said. He looked into Sophie's face and saw the horror of her expression.

Every crayon. Every single, brand-new crayon was broken into bits. Labels ripped apart. Precise, new tips dented or chipped. Every colorful stick was at least broken in half or broken into fourths. All of them. Splintered. Severed. Fractured. Split. Destroyed.

"Mr. Duke," Sophie whispered, "I don't understand."

He steadied her shaking hand with his. "Honey, I think someone's played a mean trick on you. A real mean trick, if you ask me. Do you have any idea who'd do a thing like this?"

A big teardrop ran down Sophie's cheek and landed on the broken, bottom half of her favorite color which was severed neatly between peri and winkle. "No, sir, I don't. I don't understand. Why would someone do this?"

"I don't know, sweetie. I didn't think kids could be so mean to each other, but I guess I was wrong."

A car behind the bus honked.

"Oh, be quiet!" Mr. Duke shouted loudly. "Here, honey, we'd better get you off the bus." He held the bottom of the box while Sophie replaced the lid and slipped on the rubber bands.

Honk! Honk!

Mr. Duke looked into the big, rearview mirror. "Oh, blow it out your ear," Mr. Duke answered.

Sophie turned to go down the steps. Mr. Duke always told her to have a good evening or a nice week-end, but somehow those words on this Friday afternoon didn't seem right.

"Sophie," he said, his hand still on the lever to open the door, "I'm so sorry that your crayons got broken. I really am. If I had an extra box of crayons here on the bus, I'd give them to you right now," he offered.

Sophie, looking up from the edge of the roadway, said, "Thanks, Mr. Duke." She walked around the front of the bus, checked for traffic, and hurried across the highway. The car honked again.

Mr. Duke looked into his rearview mirror. "Hold your horses," he ordered. He turned off the flashing red lights. A steady stream of oncoming cars began driving past. "You don't go, unless I go first," he said to the driver behind the bus. And ever so slowly, he put the engine into gear and inched forward.

"Crescent Moon Motel," Evan said, answering the phone later that evening.

"Is Sophie there," a voice asked.

"Yes, she is," Evan answered politely, "but she's not feeling well. Can I give her a message?"

"Oh," the voice answered. "Do you think she's going to be too sick to go to YL's birthday party tomorrow?"

"I don't know. Who is this?"

"This is Harper. Could you give her a message for me?"

"Sure. What is it?"

"Could you please tell Sophie that I bought a baseball cap with a Detroit Tigers emblem on it for YL." Harper paused for a second. "And that I'm going to be at the party, and I hope she feels well enough to come tomorrow. Okay?"

"Sure thing, Harper. I'll go and tell her right now."

"Thanks. Bye."

Evan hung up the phone and walked through the motel office into the family's living quarters. He knocked on Sophie's door.

"Come in," a small voice said.

Sophie lay on the bed, turned toward the wall.

"Hey, punkin face, you just had a call," Evan said, sitting down beside her on the edge of the twin bed.

With red-rimmed eyes, Sophie looked up at her brother. "I did?"

"Yep, it was someone named Harper. She asked me to tell you that she bought YL a baseball cap with a Detroit Tigers emblem on it."

Sophie nodded. Between getting chewed out by Mrs. TenBroeck and then the business with the crayons, she had completely forgotten about the birthday present. "I'm not going to go to YL's birthday party," she volunteered, "so it doesn't matter about the present."

"Aw, come on, Sophie, I think you ought to go."

"But what if Melody is there?" Sophie asked, rolling over and sitting up. "I'm pretty sure that either she or Suki Lufflin did it. It all had to do with being in their club. The thing is, YL invited the whole class to his birthday party. So Melody *and* Suki will probably be there."

Evan put his hand on Sophie's shoulder. "Listen to me, Sofe, think about it this way. No matter who did it, whether it was Melody or Suki, no matter who it was that busted up all your crayons, that person is a creep. A plain old, ordinary, scummy creep. And pretty soon, that creep will do another scummy thing and keep trying one rotten thing after another, but stuff like that always comes back to haunt them. Personally, I don't think that you should let one scummy person keep you from going to YL's birthday party. Being the new kid in class isn't easy. Believe me, it's no picnic at the high school. Every day, I walk up the steps into the building and I take a deep breath, trying to not let my nerves get the best of me. I keep telling myself that it's going to take some time. That I'll find someone I can do things with. It takes time to get to know people. But you can't let these two girls grind you down." Evan gave Sophie a little hug. "You'd have one friend there, anyway."

"Who?"

"Harper."

Sophie was trying not to listen anymore.

"I'll take you over to YL's party. I'll drop you off and pick you up, myself," Evan continued.

"I don't think I want to go," Sophie repeated and looked away.

Evan shook his head. "Didn't YL invite you to his party?"

"Evan, I just told you. YL invited *everyone* in the class."

"Well, didn't you tell me that YL was new this year, too?"

"Yes."

"Don't you think YL deserves a shot at having you there? Maybe he's in the same boat you're in."

"I suppose," Sophie said. "But I just had someone bust up my stuff. And . . ."

"Listen, Sofe, not more than two minutes ago, Harper called to tell you about the present she bought for the two of you to give to YL."

Sophie shrugged.

"So, what is Harper? Chopped liver?"

Sophie smiled a little bit but shrugged again. "All right, already."

"Harper sounds like an okay kid to me. At least give you and Harper and YL a chance by going to the party. Harper said she hoped you'd feel good enough to be there."

Evan stood up and ruffled Sophie's hair again. "Why don't you call her back, punkin face, and tell her you're going?"

Sophie gave a noncommittal nod. Evan left. She looked out the window and watched the first flakes of snow flutter to the ground. As the door to her bedroom clicked closed, she sighed deeply, slamming the side of her fist on the wall. "I hate being new so much," she whispered, the sick feeling returning to the pit of her stomach.

CHAPTER TWELVE

Pineapple Pizza

"The day you were born, it snowed like this," Dwayne Truax commented as he and YL pulled up at the Little Italy Pizza Parlor with noisemakers, forks, napkins, streamers, plates, tablecloths, and party hats thirty minutes before the kids were due to arrive. The smells of warm dough and spicy tomato sauce greeted them at the door. The owner, Phil Russo, showed them the corner where most everybody sat whenever there was a birthday party. YL and his father pushed together four tables, creating a big empty spot in the middle of the floor, and covered the tables with the paper birthday tablecloths. They Scotch-taped twirling strands of turquoise and lime-green crepe paper from one hanging lamp to another. YL placed a HAPPY BIRTHDAY plate, plastic fork, and hat at each place. YL's father placed the cake in the center of the four tables. It was frosted with green-and-black icing, designed to look like a replica of a football field, complete with goalposts.

YL gazed out the window. "Dad, do you think the

snow's going to keep kids from coming?" A thick layer of fluff already blanketed shrubs and trees.

His father took a quick look out the window. "I doubt it," he answered, setting extra napkin dispensers in the middle of each table as a precautionary measure. He looked at the noisemakers in the bag and decided to leave them there. He checked his watch: 5:15 P.M.

YL's father made one more trip to the car. He carried in a large carton, removing an oversize tape recorder, a black box with multiple dials and knobs, two speakers, a box of tapes, and a microphone system. He set the speakers on two opposite windowsills and plugged in the equipment. He flipped a switch on the black box.

"Testing," Dwayne Truax said into the microphone. "One. Two."

Two of the waitresses from behind the swinging doors of the kitchen poked their heads out. Phil Russo smiled and waved. The cook tasting the spaghetti sauce stopped and stared, holding the cooking spoon in midair. The busboy quit stacking dishes.

"Any special requests?" Mr. Truax called out.

"Serious?" Phil Russo shouted.

"Of course," YL's father answered. "You're the owner. You get first choice."

"That song by Roy Orbison. You know," Mr. Russo said as he took a flattened circle of pizza dough and began twirling it in the air, "the one where he sings something about making dreams come true."

"Got it," Dwayne answered.

Two cars pulled up, and two kids got out, slammed the car doors, and ran over to the entrance. Harper and Sophie hurried inside. The bells on the door handle jingled.

Dwayne Truax waved at them and flipped through his collection of cassettes. He tripped the microphone switch. His voice boomed out of the speakers.

"And now, linguine and lasagna lovers, this is Dwayne, the Dynamo, Truax, coming to you live from the Little Italy Pizza Parlor, Whispering Springs' answer to the only truly Italian cuisine this side of the Appalachian Plateau. For all you listening pepperonis out there, we're about to hear none other than Mr. Sha-la-la himself . . . Roy Orbison, dreaming sweet dreams better than anyone else I know."

YL's father flipped another switch, and the sounds of a thumping bass beat and a strumming guitar filled the restaurant.

Harper and Sophie hurried over to the birthday-party corner.

"Wow!" they said in unison.

YL pointed at them. "Jinx!" he said and then laughed.

Harper handed him a box with a frilly bow on the top. "Here. This is for you. Happy birthday."

"Here," Sophie said, "happy birthday, too."

Harper looked at her. "I thought the one present was supposed to be from both of us?"

Backup singers chanted *"Sha-la-la, sweet sha-la-la dreams"* and crooned "AAAAAAAAAHHHHHHH

. . . dream UUUUUHHHUUUUHHH baby. . . ."

"Well, the one I brought was something I thought of at the last minute," Sophie shouted above the music. "It's no big deal."

Harper and Sophie walked over to the tape player.

"Dad, this is Harper and Sophie," YL said.

Dwayne Truax extended his hand. "Hello, girls. I'll use my best radio voice for you today."

"We listen to you all the time on the school bus in the mornings," Sophie told him.

"That's good. What's your bus number? I'll play something for you on Monday."

"Number one twenty-eight," Sophie answered.

The two girls looked at each other, giving Mr. Truax embarrassed grins as they shook his hand.

"I'm taking special requests. What would you like to hear?"

Unable to decide, Sophie and Harper shrugged their shoulders.

"Maybe you'll think of something in a minute."

One of the waitresses with a bouncy blond ponytail came over to Mr. Truax. "When would you like us to have the pizzas ready?"

YL overheard the question. "Dad, do you think any more kids are going to come?" he asked.

Dwayne Truax checked his watch. "Now you've got me wondering about the weather." He turned to the waitress. "Let's wait another ten minutes. Maybe the snow is keeping some of the kids at home." He looked at the waitress's name tag. "Gloria?" he asked.

She nodded.

Mr. Truax flipped the microphone switch. *"This next song is for one of the cutest waitresses this side of the Mississippi. Let's hear it for Gloria, or better known in rock-and-roll circles as G-L-O-R-I-A."*

He stood up and asked Sophie, "How about a dance?" Sophie blushed. The two went out to the middle of the floor and began twirling and swirling. Mr. Truax motioned for YL and Harper to come out and dance, too.

Bells on the door jingled. An older couple came in. They stomped their feet, and the man knocked the snow off his wife's coat.

"If this keeps up, the interstate will be closed before long," he told Mr. Russo.

Phil showed them to a table. The couple smiled when they saw the birthday-party corner.

Mr. Truax played another record but turned down the volume a bit so the music wouldn't disturb the couple.

"Don't do that on our account," the woman said with a smile. *"We're* having a good time watching *you* have a good time."

A few minutes later, two waitresses brought five hot steamy pizzas out of the kitchen and set them on the tables.

"What are we going to do with the extra pizza, Dad? I guess nobody wanted to come to my birthday party."

"Hey, YL," Harper answered indignantly, "so what does that make us? Nobody? Aren't we somebody?"

YL wagged his head back and forth. Mr. Truax got

up and walked over to the couple and shook hands with the man. YL's father gestured toward the birthday party corner, making big circles.

The next thing YL knew, the couple was coming over.

"Wilson and Naomi Myers," the man said, extending his hand to YL. "Happy birthday, young man!" He pulled out a chair for his wife.

"Come over here, honey, and let me give you a big birthday smooch," Mrs. Myers said to YL. He grimaced as she gave him a lipsticky kiss. "I have a grandson about your age."

"Thanks," YL said, wiping off the red smear with a paper napkin. Mr. Truax changed tapes. He waved to Phil Russo, and the people from the kitchen suddenly stood around the four tables. They each put on a hat and sang to YL, with the help of a rousing tape recording of "Happy Birthday." Mr. Truax gave out the noisemakers, and Harper and Sophie gave theirs a loud blast.

"Let's eat," Mr. Truax said, offering slices of pineapple and Canadian bacon pizza to everyone. Sophie tried a piece. Harper took a slice of sausage with onions and green peppers.

YL was biting into a slice of pepperoni pizza with black olives when the bells on the door jangled. He looked up and stopped chewing. There, coming in the door, absolutely white with snow from head to toe, was an elderly gentleman. And who should step into the restaurant beside him but Mrs. TenBroeck.

YL's mouth was too full to say anything. Instead, he tapped his father on the shoulder.

The pair shook off the snow.

"For heaven's sake, Claire," Phil Russo said, walking over to them, "what are you doing out on a night like this?"

"We were on our way back from the doctor's in Morgantown," Mrs. TenBroeck said. "May I use your phone? I slid off the road about a quarter of a mile from here." She shook the snow off her coat and hooked it on the coat rack.

"That's my teacher," YL whispered in his father's ear.

"I suppose we might as well get some dinner, Dad," Mrs. TenBroeck told her father after making the phone call. "Every single tow truck is out on a call, and it's going to be awhile before they can get to us."

Mr. Truax stood up and walked over to Mrs. Ten-Broeck.

"Dad," YL called out, "what are you doing?"

Before he knew it, his father was bringing Mrs. Ten-Broeck and the older gentleman over to the table.

"Well, what do you know, YL. Happy birthday. Isn't this nice? Carl Stone, this is YL Truax," she said, pulling out a chair and guiding her father into it.

"How do you do," Mr. Stone said, eyeing the pizza. "Oh, pepperoni with black olives," he remarked. "My favorite."

"Pizza gives you heartburn, doesn't it, Dad?" Mrs. TenBroeck asked.

"Yes, but what do I care? Phil Russo makes the best pizza in town. It's worth it," he laughed. He shook hands with Mr. Truax. "Carl Stone," he said, extending his hand to the other man, "don't believe we've met."

"Wilson Myers," the man answered. "And this is my wife, Naomi." Mrs. Myers dabbed her lips with a HAPPY BIRTHDAY napkin.

"Any requests?" Mr. Truax asked Mrs. TenBroeck. She eyed the Canadian bacon and pineapple pizza and thought for a second. "I'm not up on rock-and-roll songs, but isn't there a song that goes something like dum-dum-dum-dum-dum—dum-bee-doo-bee—dum? It has kind of a fast beat to it."

"Absolutely," YL's father replied, "I'd know that one in a minute."

"For a little after-dinner dancing, Mrs. TenBroeck has a special request for 'Come and Go with Me' by the Del Vikings."

Mr. Truax stood up. "Care to have this dance, Mrs. TenBroeck?"

"Why, certainly." The pair stepped onto the makeshift dance floor.

In the middle of their dancing, Phil Russo called out from behind the counter, "Dwayne, phone for you."

"Uh, oh," YL said looking up, "there must be a problem at work. That's the only reason my father ever gets phone calls."

YL's father talked on the phone for a few minutes, then walked toward the group at the birthday table. Sure enough, YL could read the look on his father's face even before he began to speak.

"Listen, sport," YL's father began, "the boss just called and asked if I could work. Seems one of the other DJs had his car slide into a ditch and can't get to work."

"Do you have a choice whether to go or not?" YL asked.

"Not really," his father answered. "But I'm not sure how to get everyone home and get myself over to the radio station as quickly as possible."

Not more than a second later, the bells on the door jangled. Evan Spagnolo stepped into the restaurant. He stamped his feet on the rug and shook snow from his hair.

"What a koinkydink! There's your answer," Sophie volunteered. "My brother, Evan." She grabbed YL's father's hand. "Come on, Mr. Truax. I want you to meet Evan, he can give us a ride home." She walked Mr. Truax over to her brother.

"But I haven't opened my presents yet," YL moaned.

Carl Stone pushed them toward YL. "Here, young man, have a go at it. Far be it from me to say anyone kept you from your birthday presents."

YL ripped open Harper's package.

"Oh, wow!" he said, immediately putting on the Detroit Tigers hat.

"The Tigers, what a baseball team. Hank Greenberg, Al Kaline," Mr. Stone said. "Both of them great outfielders."

Evan overheard. "Yeah, but how about Denny Mc-

Clain winning thirty-one games? That was really something."

YL tugged at the ribbon on Sophie's present.

"What?" he said, holding up something long and black.

"Shake 'em out," Sophie told him.

YL gave the cloth a shake and two long, black strips tumbled down from his hand. He still looked puzzled.

"They're tights, goofus," Harper said finally.

"Oh," YL answered, "now I get it."

"They don't fit me anymore, and I thought you could use a pair of black ones. Purple's not your color, you know," Sophie teased.

"You won't mind if I don't try them on right now, will you?"

Harper laughed, turning to Mr. Truax. "Would you tell us what the YL stands for, Mr. Truax?" she asked. "YL won't. He says wild horses couldn't drag it out of him."

Mr. Truax shook his head and winked at his son. "Nope. I won't divulge the secret either, not unless I get the okay from YL."

"Yale Locks," Mr. Stone guessed. "That would be my guess, but I was a locksmith in the Navy. That's the first thing I thought of," he added. "Yale Locks," he repeated.

"Nope, not even close," YL said.

"Here," Mr. Truax said, handing Sophie a length of cable to coil, "we'll have to start packing everything."

Dwayne Truax unplugged cords and cables from his

equipment. One of the waitresses wrapped the leftover pizza in aluminum foil. Evan carried a speaker out to Mr. Truax's car. The birthday-party corner was returned to its normal pizza-parlor condition.

YL, Harper, and Mrs. TenBroeck smooshed into the backseat of the Spagnolo station wagon. Evan, Mr. Stone, and Sophie sat in the front seat and peered into the fuzzy whiteness of the snowstorm. The wipers whamped-whamped as the headlights cast bands of yellow light into the fluttering flakes. The car crept along the highway. They passed Mrs. TenBroeck's automobile, mired up to the axles in the ditch. Everyone leaned forward, squinty-eyed. The station wagon was the only car traveling along the road.

"Turn left," Mr. Stone said, two blocks from the motel.

Sophie was surprised to see Mrs. TenBroeck's house was so close to hers.

When Evan pulled into the Stones's driveway, the drifts were up to the hubcaps.

"Don't get snow like this very often in West Virginia," Mr. Stone told Evan. "Makes me want to go out and build a snowman."

Mrs. TenBroeck laughed. "Come on, Dad, don't get too carried away." She opened the door. "Happy birthday, YL. And thanks for the lift, Evan. You're a lifesaver."

YL, Harper, and Sophie gazed into the fluffy darkness, trying to get a better view of where Mrs. TenBroeck lived. Sophie rubbed a circle on the steamy window. She made a fist and pressed the side of her hand onto the misty glass, leaving an imprint. She used her index finger to make five dots along the top. By the time she was finished, the image of a baby's foot appeared on the window of the side door.

"Don't forget your homework," Mrs. TenBroeck said, getting ready to slam the door shut. "And don't forget your permission slips."

"Listen to her," Mr. Stone added with a smile. "Once a teacher, always a teacher." He turned to YL. "Thanks for the heartburn, young man. That's the best pizza I've had in a long time."

Mrs. TenBroeck and her father trudged through the snow.

"Leave it to our teacher to remind us about homework," Harper said.

"And ruin our weekend," YL added.

"Yes, but we can always pray for a snow day," Sophie said, and on that note, everyone began to shout "Snow day! Snow day!" and bounce up and down in their seats until the car looked like a popcorn popper ready to explode.

CHAPTER THIRTEEN

Chicken Feathers, Hope, and Faith

"If I were you," Harper said as she, Sophie, and YL walked back from the art room, "I'd go right over and tell Melody Briscoe what a jerk she is."

"I can't do that," Sophie answered. "Besides, I'm not sure it was Melody who busted up the crayons."

"Geez louise, Sophie! Who do you think did it? The good fairy?" YL said. "Those crayons didn't jump out of the box on their own and get broken."

Sophie didn't say anything.

"What did your mom say when you told her?" Harper asked.

"I didn't tell her. I went into my room and stayed there. I told her I had a stomachache."

"You didn't tell her?" YL asked with disbelief.

"No, I didn't tell my parents, and I made Evan swear he wouldn't say anything."

Harper smacked herself in the forehead with the palm of her hand. "Sofe," Harper said, beginning to pace back and forth in the hallway, "you could've gotten your mother to call Melody's mother . . ."

"For what?"

"For . . . for," Harper began. "I don't know, maybe to get her in trouble."

Sophie stopped walking and said, "I suppose, but Melody doesn't look like the kind of kid that gets into trouble. You know kids like Melody."

YL thought for a second. "Yeah, I suppose you're probably right. When Melody gets into trouble, her mother taps the back of her hand and says something like"—YL changed his voice so that it was high-pitched—"'Now Melody, dear, naughty, naughty. Breaking little Sophie's crayons. For shame. For shame.' "

Sophie smiled.

"Wow," Harper said with relief. "I thought for a minute the old smiler on the front of your face was never going to work again."

As they neared the room, they heard Mrs. TenBroeck's voice drift into the hallway. "Clear off your desks. We have just enough time for Chapter Four from the book."

"Are you going to do anything to Melody?" YL asked.

Sophie's eyes grew as big as fifty-cent pieces. "No," she said. "Maybe Melody didn't even do it."

"Oh, don't give me that boloney! Of course she did it. Or else one of her henchmen like Suki Lufflin did!" Harper said.

"Well, all right. Maybe they *were* the ones. It really makes me mad that they broke every single crayon, but . . ."

Harper grasped the doorknob and whispered to Sophie and YL, "But, nothing. Listen, Sofe, leave it to me. I'll see what I can do to even up the score. You know what I always say. Don't get mad," she offered, pulling open the door for the three of them.

"Get even!" YL finished for her.

"Right," Harper said, giving YL the thumbs-up sign.

Sophie and YL watched as Harper strolled into the classroom and smiled a great, big, devilish grin at Melody Briscoe.

Mrs. TenBroeck looked over her bifocals and stopped reading. She waited for Sophie, YL, and Harper to sit down. Once they were seated, Mrs. Ten-Broeck continued.

Lying on my side on a woven mat, I kept careful watch on an opening between the ice floes. I bobbed two pieces of ivory jigging on the end of a seal-hide line. My fingers tingled from the vibrations of a nibbling fish. Spear ready, I moved swiftly, silently. Jab! Missed! Jab! Missed again!

"Aaah," I muttered, annoyed with myself for letting such a big, tender fish get away. I thought of the only food in our igloo, the few mataq flakes left in the skin bag hanging on the wall. My catch of fish would let us save the dried flakes of whale skin for another time.

The wind whistled past my shoulders. I pushed back

my hood to hear more clearly. Were those the sounds
of strong winds coming down from the north? The
strong winds bringing a drifter? The strong winds
which brought the blinding, smoking snow and the
bitterest cold?

Apoppa licked my neck and I returned my concentration to fishing. When the afternoon light began to
flatten, I knew I would need to leave enough time to
make my way back to the igloo before the darkness of
night.

Wait. What was that? A silver shimmer, deep in the
water. The tingling of a nibble. I prepared myself.
Spear ready. Keep the fin in sight. Steady.

Now! Jab! A wild, wriggling fish jerked and flipped
on the end of my spear.

"Aiyee!" I shouted, hauling the fish out of the water. Its mouth opened and closed. Its body thumped
and twisted on the ice.

Cold winds bit through my gloves as I strung
the fish through the open end of my spear and balanced the long pole on my shoulder. I leaned forward into the gusting wind, and with every step
toward our igloo, the fish bumped against my back.
But I did not care. My thoughts were only on the
fish we would have for dinner. Exciting thoughts.
Good thoughts. My thoughts of dream food had
come true. The treacherous walk home in the half-
light went quickly. I took no notice of the strength-
ening wind.

I noticed nothing unusual, that is, until I reached
the last rise before our igloo. Apoppa whimpered. A
sound had reached her ears. Before I could turn to put

my hand over her mouth to quiet her, she gave another whimper. Then I heard the sound, too.

Rooooar! Again, even louder. *ROOAAR!*

There was no mistaking the crazed sounds of a polar bear. I ran for shelter. Luckily I was downwind. The polar bear had not caught our scent with the drifter blowing past me. What was I to do? One small child against a mighty polar bear.

I crawled a few feet on my hands and knees to look over the rise. I lifted my head ever so slightly, and became even more frightened, more terrified, for what I saw left me feeling helpless. The polar bear was attacking our camp. He paced back and forth. There was a wild look in his eyes. Perhaps he'd gone mad. Two dogs Father had left behind were ripped apart, their blood covering the snow like a blanket. I made myself look past the dead bodies to our igloo. My heart nearly stopped beating.

Steps Softly, I thought. Grandmother, I whispered to myself. The bear, with its wild strength, had thrown its weight against the walls again and again, caving in one side. A tumbled mound of ice blocks was the only thing left.

The bear roared and roared, lumbering back and forth.

Apoppa whimpered. The bear tipped its head, sniffed the air, and looked in our direction. As he stopped to inspect his paw, I thought of a plan. When the bear's back was turned to us, I took my catch of fish by the tail and hurled it with all my might in the bear's direction. The bear spotted it.

Wild and frothing at the mouth, the bear grabbed

the fish with one of its mighty paws, turned, and ran away from me.

Crouching low, I hurried to our igloo. In the growing darkness, I stumbled and stepped over the broken walls.

"Grandmother?" I called. "Steps Softly?" There was no answer. Using my hands, I tried moving the heavy blocks. A large section of the roof had collapsed under the bear's weight. Beneath that section, I found Grandmother. I touched her face, but knew at once that she was dead.

"Steps Softly?" I called. There was a faint cry from the opposite side of the destroyed igloo.

Pushing blocks of snow aside and throwing my weight against others, I moved several until I found Steps Softly wedged against an inside wall, her tiny, freezing hands reaching out for me. I held her to me, brushing the snow from her cheeks, her little fingers tightly clutching the fur of my parka. My mind raced with questions. What to do? Where to go? What to take for our survival?

A tiny yap came from the small shelter for the pups. Steps Softly pointed toward the wall. I sliced an opening with my knife. Tiintuk ran out, nearly jumping into my arms.

All around us, the drifter blew more steadily and the first wisps of smoking snow skimmed along the ground. In that instance, I realized what I must do.

"We are going now," I told Steps Softly. "I know an abandoned igloo not far from here. We can stay there for the night."

I bundled her inside my jacket, nestled the two pups

into a seal-hide bag, and found the cache of mataq chips under some snow blocks. I grabbed two caribou skins, the small bundle with the soapstone lamp, pot, and soaking moss, and a bag with a small box of toys for Steps Softly.

By moonlight, I dusted my footprints as I backed away from the igloo. I did this task carefully, for I wanted no dead spirits to follow us. Even though I had touched Grandmother's face with my hand, and I knew I should leave the mitten which had touched her, I broke with ritual and kept it on for my protection.

Steps Softly clung to my neck. I patted her back and offered her comforting words. I looked into the darkness, saw a sky filled with stars beyond counting, and thought only of our survival.

Mrs. TenBroeck closed the book. The clock buzzed, signaling the end of the day. "Wednesday's the last day for permission slips," she reminded her students. "And we'll start working on our dioramas. We need some decent-looking exhibits for Parents' Night, so put on your thinking caps, my little sled dogs."

YL answered the phone's second ring. "Hello."

"Is this my baby boy?"

YL smiled. "Mom, how come you keep calling me your baby boy? I'm twelve years old now."

"I know that, but I can't help myself," Denise Truax answered. "How was your party?"

"It was okay," YL replied. "We had a big snow-storm. Not many kids showed up."

"Oh, that's too bad. Did you get many presents?"

"Well, Dad gave me a telescope. And two of my friends gave me a Detroit Tigers hat." YL didn't mention the tights.

There was a pause on the other end of the phone before YL's mother spoke again. He could hear muffled voices in the background.

"I'm sorry I didn't call you on your birthday, sweetie, but the weekend was a little hectic."

"That's okay."

"We were a little busy."

"We?"

"Yes, Phillip and I."

"Oh."

There was another pause.

"YL?"

"Yes, Mom." YL heard his mother's hand go over the mouthpiece of the phone.

"YL, I want to talk to you about something. I have some pretty exciting news to tell you. We thought maybe we'd wait awhile before we told you, but we decided to break the news to everyone, and we wanted you to be the first to hear it."

"Oh, what is it?" YL heard his mother's hand go over the mouthpiece again.

A man's voice suddenly came on the line. "Hello?"

"Who is this?"

"Hi, YL. This is Phillip. You don't know me yet,

but your mother and I have been seeing each other. I'm looking forward to meeting you."

"Oh."

"Your mother wanted me to say hello."

"Hello."

Static crackled on the phone line.

"Well, I'll put her back on."

For a third time, YL's mother put her hand over the mouthpiece.

"YL? Are you ready for the good news?"

"Yeah, Mom."

"YL, honey, Phillip and I are getting married."

"Oh."

"Isn't that wonderful?"

There was a long pause on YL's end of the phone. "Sure, Mom. That's nice."

"YL, you don't sound very enthusiastic."

"I'm enthusiastic, Mom. See, I'm smiling."

His mother laughed. "YL, you're such a funny kid."

"How soon?"

"How soon, what?"

"How soon are you getting married?"

There was another pause. Denise Truax cleared her throat. "Next weekend."

YL shook his head. "Oh," he replied.

"I know this is kind of sudden, honey, but Phillip and I are both very excited. Matter-of-fact, for your birthday present we're going to send you a ticket to fly to Detroit over Easter vacation so you and Phillip can meet each other."

"Oh."

"You can meet Phillip's two daughters."

"He has kids?"

"Yes, Phillip has two girls. But they won't live with us. They'll live with his ex-wife."

"Oh."

"Won't that be fun, YL? You'll finally have some sisters."

"I suppose." YL yawned.

"Tired, honey?"

"Yeah, a little bit."

Static sputtered across the line again.

"Well, sweetie, I guess I'd better go. I'm glad you had such a nice birthday."

"Yep," YL said. "Thanks for calling, Mom."

"Sure do love you, sweetie."

"I love you, too, Mom."

"I'll talk to you soon."

"Talk to you soon."

"Bye-bye."

"Bye, Mom."

As YL hung up the phone, his father came into the room.

"How's Mom?" he asked.

"Fine."

"Anything new with Mom in scenic Detroit?"

YL looked away, shrugging his shoulders, then muttered, "Nope, not a single, solitary thing."

"That's good, 'cause I've got a surprise for you," his father said. He stood by the front door. "Grab your coat, we're going to take a little ride. I want you to meet someone. I think I've found the perfect person for you to stay with while I'm working late."

YL shuffled slowly over to the closet. "Oh, phooey!" he mumbled under his breath.

Harper peeled carrots at the sink while her mother made a sandwich to eat between evening classes. "Mrs. TenBroeck wants me to ask if you will, pretty please, with sugar on it, try and find my baby book."

She couldn't see the look on her mother's face. "I think it was probably misplaced in one of our moves," her mother answered. "I already looked for it the other night after you asked, Harper."

Slivers of orange carrot peelings slid into the sink. Harper slipped carrot sticks into a silver mixing bowl.

"Everyone filled in their family-history time lines today. Everyone but me. Mine looked like I was an orphan."

"Orphans have no parents. You've got me," Harper's mother reminded.

Harper rolled her eyes. "Oh, Mom! I couldn't put in anything about Dad's side of the family. How about his mother and father? Don't I have grandparents from Dad's side of the family?"

"Probably, but we lost touch years ago."

"What's their name? I could call and ask them about my cousins and aunts and uncles." Harper munched on a carrot as she talked. "Harold Pon found out that he still has a whole slew of relatives in Taiwan. His mom actually called an uncle in Taipei to check on something so Harold could put it on his chart."

"Good for Harold, but it doesn't work like that for you, Harper. You simply can't pick up the telephone and call people out of the blue. At least not from your father's family."

"Mom, I promise I won't say anything about Dad being dead in case it would make them sad. What's their name? What city do they live in?"

Harper's mother turned and looked at her. "Harp, do me a favor and give it a rest." The sound of carrots being scraped filled the room. "I do wish you would have had the chance to meet my parents. My mother was a really fun person, but she died when she was so young. Her name was Jean. You're . . ." Harper's mother cut the sandwich in half, but stopped. "My dad was a wonderful person, too."

"How'd they die?"

"Well, with my mother, it was cancer," Harper's mother said. "Mom had breast cancer. She was in and out of the hospital and sick for maybe two months. I remember she was very weak and really, really thin. And then suddenly, she was dead. I always knew she was sick, but I never dreamed she'd die. You don't think much about your mom dying when you're a kid. At least I didn't."

"Do you remember her funeral, Mom?"

"Oh, sure, honey. There's no way in the world I

could ever forget something like that." Harper's mother stopped peeling carrots again. "My father and I stood there at the funeral home. Well, I stood up, but they had to get a chair for my dad because he had to sit down. He was so broken up over my mother dying like that. Her funeral lasted for two days and by the end of those two days, my father had changed right before my very eyes."

Harper put her arm around her mother's waist.

"We buried my mother on a Monday. In July. Mercy, it was hot. I remember that as clear as anything," she continued. "And the following week, I buried my father."

Harper remembered hearing her mother talk about this once before. She hugged her mom again. She asked the next question, although she thought she knew the answer. "What'd he die of?"

"People in town said he died of a broken heart."

"A broken heart? How can you die of a broken heart, Mom?"

"I don't know for sure, sweetie, but when my mother died, it was like something inside my father shut down and died, too. When he didn't show up for breakfast two days after we'd buried my mother, I went into his room to wake him, and I found him dead in his bed."

"Was that when you were sent to live with Aunt Ruthie and Uncle Minot in Tacoma?"

Harper's mother answered in a way that let Harper know she didn't want to talk about the next part.

"Was that when you ran away?" she asked anyway.

Her mother began peeling the carrots very quickly. "Enough of this business, Harper."

"How old were you?"

"Too young to have any good sense and old enough to know better."

"Was that when you met Dad? How old were you when you and Dad were married?"

"What is this, a quiz show?"

"No, but I just want to know this stuff, that's all."

"Sixteen going on thirty-five, or so I thought."

"Then you were only seventeen when you had me."

"Well, I've always figured that I should tell you the truth about that, because once you were old enough to count on your fingers, I knew you'd figure it out for yourself. You're twelve. My driver's license says I'm twenty-nine, so that means you were born when I was seventeen."

"Where'd you meet Dad?"

"He was stationed at a military base outside of Tacoma."

"Did you go out for a long time?"

"Not too long. Your father served two tours of duty in Vietnam."

"Was he tall and handsome? And . . ."

"Twenty questions is over, Harp."

"Why do we always stop talking when it comes to the parts about Dad?"

Caroline Stritch turned away.

"Did he love me? Did he like to play with me? Did he bounce me on his knee and play Trot-Trot-to-

Boston with me? Was I a little pain-in-the-neck when I was a kid?"

"You're a pain-in-the neck now. Enough of this, already, Harper. I've got to get to class."

"You know, Mom, I only want to hear about him. I don't even know my father's middle name. What was it?"

Harper's mother put her arm through one of the straps on her backpack. She thought for a second.

"Don't you remember his middle name?"

"Of course I remember his name," she answered smartly, but she spoke the next part of the sentence slowly. "His middle name was Lee." She turned and started out the door, hurrying down the steps. "Keep the door locked. Don't let anybody in. Stay off the phone. I'll be home late. You can watch TV after you finish your homework. And don't forget to feed Jupiter." She disappeared around the corner, leaving Harper standing in the middle of the landing.

"Ronald Lee Stritch," she whispered. "I have the same middle name as my father."

Jupiter poked her nose out the door.

"Oh, no, you don't," Harper said. "Back, Sheba, back!" Harper ordered, pretending she had a whip in her hand like an animal tamer in a circus. Harper scooped the cat into her arms. "You know, Jupiter, I'd really like to know what my father looked like. My homework's done. There's nothing good on TV." Harper kissed the cat on the head, right between the ears. "What do you say we look for my baby book tonight?"

Jupiter's answer was a steady purr, purr, purring noise from deep within her throat.

Sophie couldn't believe her eyes when she saw YL and his father pull into the parking lot of the Crescent Moon Motel.

"Are they here?" Mrs. Spagnolo asked, coming out of the office.

Sophie looked at her mother. "Did you know they were coming?"

"Sure, I invited them," she explained.

YL and his father came into the office.

"Hey, YL, what are you doing here?" Sophie asked.

"Beats me," he answered.

"Mrs. Spagnolo," Dwayne Truax said.

"It's nice to meet you," Mrs. Spagnolo replied, shaking his hand. "Why don't you come into the kitchen?" she said, motioning toward a long hallway.

YL looked at Sophie. Sophie looked at YL. They both shook their heads.

Mrs. Spagnolo removed a calendar from the refrigerator and sat down at the kitchen table. "Now, what nights will YL be staying with us?" she asked.

"I'm staying here, with Sophie?" YL questioned.

"Mom, you're kidding," Sophie said. "YL's going to stay at our house?"

"Sure," Mrs. Spagnolo answered, "what's one more when you run a motel?"

"Yep, this is your new Miss McPurtle," Dwayne Truax explained. "When I called to thank Sophie's mother and Evan for giving you a ride home from the birthday party, we got to talking and came up with this solution. Mrs. Spagnolo doesn't even look like Miss McPurtle, does she, YL?"

YL laughed. He could see by Mrs. Spagnolo's smile that she didn't have false teeth.

"Come on," Sophie told YL, "I'll show you the pool table." She started down the steps to the family room. "I've never had a boy stay over at my house before."

YL grabbed her arm and stopped her. "You're sworn to secrecy about this, okay, Sophie? No one knows. Promise me."

"You can count on me, YL. I won't tell a living person, scout's honor."

Lana got up off the couch and walked over to YL. "Hi, what's your name?"

"YL," he said, looking at the top of her hair which had been neatly parted and pulled into two ponytails.

"That's your name?" she asked.

"Oh, brother," YL answered.

Lana took YL's hand and led him over to the couch. "I want you to sit by me." She pulled on his arm so that he couldn't do anything but sit down. "We can play Sweetie Bears together," she explained, handing him a plastic bear with glowing green hair and wild, pop-out eyes.

"Hey, little sister," Sophie interrupted, "YL's down here to play pool with me."

"Oh, brother," YL mumbled, looking from Sophie to Lana.

"I get him," Lana ordered.

"No, he's my friend. He's here to play pool with me," Sophie argued.

"Girls!" YL muttered, rolling his eyes back. "I guess I'd better get used to this."

CHAPTER FOURTEEN

The Wall

At 6:04 A.M., two orange school buses waited in the Whispering Springs Elementary School parking lot, their engines running, heaters blasting. Parents dropped off their sixth graders and gave last-minute instructions. A few mothers and fathers stood and waited to wave good-bye as the buses pulled away. Mr. Duke switched on the radio dial to 91.6 as the bus rumbled down the entrance to the interstate.

YL smiled when he heard his father's voice.

The kids were chattering to each other until suddenly, Bobby Ray shouted, "Hey, shut up and listen. It's YL's dad on the radio and he's talking about us!"

"Rumor has it, there's a group of wild-and-woolly sixth graders from Whispering Springs Elementary School on their way to the nation's capital today. So I thought I'd play a little traveling music for them this morning. This next song is dedicated to all their brave teachers and chaperones and in particular, Aloo and

Carnell and Sophie and Melody and Suki and Charles and Amanda and Stephanie and Martin." Everyone on the school bus heard Dwayne, the Dynamo, take a very deep breath. *"And Crosby and Harper and Steve and Rayna and Sunday and Bobby Ray and Christa and Loren and Emily and Harold and Carla. And . . . my main man, YL. Have a great time today, kids. Stay out of trouble and say hello to Mr. President for me just in case you happen to see him. All you kids on old one twenty-eight, cruisin' along and playin' the radio, and that means you, too, Mr. Duke, this one's for you"*—a twangy guitar did the leadoff as Chuck Berry began to sing. The kids on the bus shouted and clapped.

Before Cooper's Rock, kids began wadding up their jackets for pillows and leaning heads on each other's shoulders. Twenty miles outside of Cumberland, Maryland, most everyone was sound asleep. Three and a half hours later, Mrs. TenBroeck stood up and clapped her hands. "Wake up! I want to get some of your red, white, and blue patriotic blood flowing. I won't have you sleep your way through Washington, D.C.!"

She marched the class up the front steps of the National Museum of American History, through the big heavy doors, past the rotunda's trumpeting elephant and directly into the hallway of Native Cultures of the Americas.

"Now this," she announced triumphantly, "is what we've trekked all the way to Washington to see!" Students with wide-eyed stares stood motionless in the middle of the hallway. "Get out paper and pencils. Start taking notes. Jot things down. Get some ideas for your dioramas from these scenes," she advised, pointing to a ceremonial hunting mask. "I want to see you writing about the little details you find," she added, directing everyone's attention to the life-size statues of five Inuit hunters with their dogs watching the capture of a small seal.

Sophie knelt beside the exhibit, jotting notes from one of the displays showing Inuit children's miniature carved toys. "Look," Sophie told YL, "there's a soapstone lamp, like the one Stars kept burning all night." YL faced the adjacent case and tried his hand at sketching a long caribou robe worn by one of the men in a clothing exhibit.

Harper had a different goal in mind. She remained in the hallway, studying the floor plan of the National Museum of American History, wondering which entrance was better, the Constitution Avenue or the Mall entrance for a quick escape. She didn't want to waste a moment, since timing would be everything.

"Meet me by the elephants," Harper whispered to Sophie as the groups were divided. One set of students was herded toward the corridor of Asian Cultures while the other group went toward the Earth, Moon, and Meteorites exhibit.

"Why?"

"Don't ask why, just do it."

Sophie shook her head. "Not unless you tell me why."

Harper closed her eyes and clenched her hands into fists. "Because I need you to help me with something."

"What?"

"Come on, Sofe, do you have to give me the third degree about everything?"

Sophie looked toward the rest of the students in the class walking down the corridor. "All right, already. I'll do it, but I want to know why. I don't see what's so wrong with wanting to know why I'm doing something."

"Because it's my only chance."

"Chance? What chance?"

"To see for myself. To see The Wall."

"What wall?"

"The memorial wall for the Vietnam veterans. At least I could see my father's name. My mother would probably never bring me here to see it."

"Is it across the street?"

"Sort of."

"What do you mean, sort of?"

"It's down the block a little."

"You mean we're going to leave the museum and go to The Wall?"

Harper nodded, and Sophie shook her head.

"Harper, that's crazy. We don't even know where it is. Maybe it's a long way from here. What if we get lost? What if we can't get back in time? Holy moley, Harper, this is nuts."

"No, it's not, Sophie, it's my only chance. If we go during lunch, no one will miss us."

"You mean, we'd miss lunch?"

"Listen to me, Sophie, we won't miss lunch. I promise you won't miss a chance to eat. The classes are going to get split up for lunch and the teachers and chaperones will probably lose track of what kids are with which teacher."

"What if we get mugged or something?"

"Sofe, we're not going to get mugged. It's broad daylight in the middle of Washington, D.C."

Sophie could see the students in her group moving farther and farther away from her toward the Asian Cultures exhibit.

"It's up to you, Sofe," Harper said finally. "If you're going to go with me, make some excuse when the others are going downstairs for lunch, like having to use the bathroom, and come back up here and meet me at the elephant. We can always get a hot dog from one of the street vendors. Their booths were lined up outside when we were getting off the buses. We'll hustle over to The Wall and be back before anyone even realizes we're missing."

Sophie looked at Harper. Sophie had never seen her appear so alive. So energized. So hopeful.

"Oh, okay, I'll go with you."

"That's great. See if you can get YL to come, too," Harper said as she turned and ran down the right-hand corridor before Sophie could say anything more. Sophie hurried down the left-hand corridor, running past the Plains Indians exhibits, trying to catch up with the others, but not wanting to draw attention to herself.

"Excuse me, officer, could you tell us how to get to The Wall?" Harper asked, stepping up to a man in a policeman's uniform.

"Honey, I'm not a policeman, I'm a security guard. I work here at the museum," he explained. "Do you mean the Vietnam Veterans Memorial?"

"Yes, sir. That's what I mean."

He turned toward the busy street. "Well, that's easy," he replied, " 'cause you can walk there from here. It's at the end of this long grassy park area called the Mall." He eyed the children for the first time.

"We're doing family histories, and I have to find my father's name. Different groups of kids are going to different areas. We have The Wall." Harper motioned toward herself, YL, and Sophie.

"See that big thing sticking up into the sky over there?" He squatted down and pointed with his index finger. She nodded. "That's the Washington Monument. You walk yourselves right past that and keep on going. Stay on the right-hand side." He pulled a small map out of his pocket and opened it up. He pointed as he explained the next part. "Cross Seventeenth Street, and be careful. That's going to be a big, busy street. As you walk toward the Lincoln Memorial, stay on the right side of the Reflecting Pool. At the end of the pool, make a big, right turn. You'll see the booth for the Vietnam Veterans Memorial. It's low in the ground. You might not spot it right off."

"Someone told me that all the names of the men who died in Vietnam are listed on it. Is that right?" Harper asked.

The guard nodded. "Women's names, too," he added.

Harper turned in the direction the guard had pointed. She shoved the map into her coat pocket.

"Thanks," Harper said, grabbing YL's and Sophie's hands and pulling them down the steps by the big stone lions.

Sophie could barely catch her breath as they approached the Vietnam Veterans Memorial Information Booth. "I thought you said we'd get to eat our lunch." She pushed at the stitch in her side, hoping it would go away.

"We can eat when we get back," Harper answered.

"She must live on air," YL said with annoyance. "I'm really going to be hungry."

Breathlessly, Harper explained what she wanted to know to the female park ranger at the green-and-white-roofed information booth. "I'm looking for my father's name. How do I find it on The Wall?"

The ranger pointed toward a small librarylike stand by the sidewalk. "Look in the directory. First, you find the name, then you find the panel the name is on. Every panel is numbered. The first casualties are listed on Panel Number One, where the two walls meet."

Harper ran to the book without waiting for the ranger to finish.

"Thank you," Sophie said.

"Maybe your friend might want to have this," the ranger added. YL took the small gray-and-black brochure the ranger held out to him.

By the time Sophie and YL reached Harper, she was already flipping through the pages.

Sophie continued walking down the pathway toward the point in the memorial where the two walls came together.

"It looks like a phone book," YL told Harper, noticing the small print on the guide. He looked up as the blast of a jet engine sounded overhead.

"Strippoli," Harper read aloud. "Stritt-mater," she pronounced slowly. "Strizzi." She looked up. "There's no Stritch. How can that be? There's no Stritch."

"Maybe he was missing in action?"

"No, his name would be listed."

"Is Bobby Ray's uncle on there?"

"What's his name?"

"Well, Bobby Ray's last name is McKinnon. The name must be something, something McKinnon," YL answered.

Harper flipped to the middle of the book. "Look! There's Bobby Ray McKinnon. Do you suppose that's it?"

"Could be," YL answered.

Sophie ran back to Harper and YL. "Did you find your father's name?"

Harper shook her head.

"Come and see what I found," Sophie offered. "I can't believe it."

"Did you find my father's name?" Harper asked, but Sophie didn't answer.

The three children hurried down the path. They moved past an older couple taking a picture of a long stone panel. Another man, dressed in camouflage pants, reached out and gently rubbed his fingertips along a name. A woman and a little girl left a bouquet of red and white carnations tied with a wide blue ribbon between the wall and the stone walkway.

"It's here," Sophie said, pointing toward the top of a shiny black panel.

"My father's name?" Harper asked.

"No," Sophie replied. "I found one of the women's names. Up there, toward the top. Do you see it?" she explained, pointing to the top of the panel numbered 1W. "Mary Therese Klinker," Sophie said. They squinted.

"I see it," YL answered finally.

"Me, too," Harper said. "But how come my father's name isn't here? Maybe I can go ask one of the rangers to help me look."

YL checked his watch. "Geez louise," he said, "we don't have time to do anything like that." He tapped the face of his watch. "We'll be late as it is. They're going to be looking for us, for sure."

"How do we get back?" Sophie asked.

"The same way we got here," YL offered, grabbing her hand and starting to run. "Come on, Harper."

Harper stood on the path, staring at the panels and panels of thousands and thousands of names stretching to her right and left along both sides of the black walls.

"He's not here," she said aloud. "I don't understand. Why isn't my father's name here? It's supposed to be here, but it's not."

"Harper!" YL hollered. He and Sophie had already gone quite a distance away from her.

Harper turned and ran toward them. The three children never stopped until they reached Seventeenth Street. They waited breathlessly to cross the busy intersection.

With an edge of annoyance to her voice, Sophie said, "I wish we could've gotten some lunch. I'm starving."

They ran across the street.

Harper still hadn't said anything, but when Sophie turned to look at her, her irritation changed to sympathy. Sophie suddenly felt a strange ache in her chest. Harper was crying.

"We're the lucky duckies," YL whispered to Sophie and Harper who fell in line with the other students stepping onto the idling school bus. Mrs. TenBroeck walked quickly toward them. She had a no-nonsense look on her face.

"Maybe not," Sophie replied, trying to hide behind Stephanie Grissom.

"Where on earth have you been? We've had everyone looking for you," Mrs. TenBroeck scolded.

Sophie tried to gather her thoughts.

"We . . ." she began, "Harper wanted to go back to see the dinosaur exhibit."

YL came to Sophie's rescue. "Sophie and I wanted to go downstairs to the museum store. We got lost and went to the store on the second floor. We were over by the gems and minerals exhibit . . ."

Mrs. TenBroeck stopped YL in midsentence. "Enough, enough," she said, waving them into a seat and sounding exasperated. "Do me a humongous favor and put your little fannies down in that seat and don't leave your groups until we get back to Whispering Springs."

She clapped her hands. The bus lurched forward. "Next stop, the Smithsonian," she announced.

On the way home, Harper sat next to the window. Sophie noticed that the tears were gone, but salt streaks showed on Harper's face where the wetness had trailed down her cheeks. Harper leaned her head against the glass and closed her eyes.

Sophie's stomach grumbled and rumbled. YL slept. Harper barely spoke a word. By the time the bus crossed the state line into West Virginia, Harper had lost her sad look and a new kind of radiance surrounded her. Sophie shuddered, knowing Harper's determination came from a need to find out the real reason Ronald

Lee Stritch's name was not listed among those on the Vietnam Veterans Memorial.

As YL and Sophie stood in the parking lot waiting to be picked up, they watched Harper run over to her mother's VW and begin asking questions as she opened the door, then slammed it angrily after she got in.

"What do you think she's going to say to her mom?" Sophie remarked.

"Don't know," YL answered, exhaling a sigh of relief. "I'm just thankful it's not me in that car."

CHAPTER FIFTEEN

Signs Point to Yes

"Harper Lee Stritch?" Mrs. Dildine asked, a silver whistle dangling from her neck. Only her head stuck through the doorway of Room 17. "I still don't have any immunization records for her," she told Mrs. Ten-Broeck. Sophie looked up. Her head ached from working on a page of story problems for math.

"Harper's not here this morning," Mrs. TenBroeck answered.

"I wonder where Harper is?" YL whispered to Sophie during TNT.

Sophie threw her hands in the air and shrugged. "Don't know," she replied.

Right after lunch and halfway through science class, Harper showed up for school.

"Did we have a little trouble getting out of bed this morning?" Mrs. TenBroeck asked.

Harper scowled. "No. *We* didn't have any trouble getting out of bed this morning. I'm late, that's all."

Eyeing Harper, Mrs. TenBroeck took off her bifocals. "Sounds to me like you got up on the *wrong* side of the bed."

She gave Harper the instructions for the work she had missed. "Mrs. Dildine wants to see you. Something about your health records," Mrs. TenBroeck reminded.

"Yeah, right," Harper said, walking toward her seat.

Sophie looked up as her friend sat down and took out her math book. Harper stared at the chalkboard, tapping her pencil on her head. Eventually, she looked at Sophie and raised her index finger in silent greeting.

"Open the windows," Mrs. TenBroeck said, reaching for *Children of the Northern Lights* fifteen minutes before gym.

"Oh, no," Christa moaned, "here we go again." She stood up and headed into the cloakroom for her coat.

"Sit down, Christa. I think you can live with a little bit of nip in the air," Mrs. TenBroeck commanded. "Draw down the blinds, Emily. And, Steve, please turn off the lights. Everyone, move back to the reading corner." Some students pushed desks aside, others merely turned around. A few children sat on the floor. The cold air seemed to follow them.

The room suddenly took on a dark, eerie, gray light. Mrs. TenBroeck slipped on her bifocals. "Now, where were we?" she asked, running the class through half a dozen questions about Stars and the story. When she seemed satisfied that they remembered enough of the details, she took out her bookmark and placed it on the desk.

Chapter Five: Bitter cold and the promise of starlight surrounded us that night in the abandoned igloo I remembered and found. I had walked for more than two hours. I was nearing exhaustion by the time we stopped. All around us, the drifter howled. Wisps of smoking snow blew in between the cracks of the deteriorating walls.

"You were such a brave girl," I told Steps Softly. Her big brown eyes searched mine. While we had traveled to the igloo, she had held onto my neck, gently but tightly, which had made the walking easier.

"Tonight is a two-dog night," I told my tiny sister as I nestled her between two layers of caribou skins, placing a puppy on either side of her. She lay on her stomach. The puppies licked her face, hoping to share a bite of the mataq chip I had given her.

I pulled the caribou skin carefully around her shoulders and reached into my pocket for the extra fishing line I put there earlier in the morning. I knotted it, making a circle of string. Steps Softly smiled, for she knew I would tell her a story.

"Once, there was a young Netsilik hunter," I said, looping the string onto my fingers, "who set out in his kayak to catch a seal."

Steps Softly's eyes followed every move of my fingers.

"When he came upon a giant ice floe," I said, dropping a string, "he circled the floe once, twice, then a third time," I explained, twisting the string on my index finger each time. "And at last he spotted a seal."

Her eyes widened.

"This young hunter quietly pulled his kayak onto the ice floe, but as he stepped out with one foot, he dropped his bow." Saying that, I let go of one of the strings. Her eyes grew bigger. "And as he stepped out onto the ice floe with the other foot, he dropped his hunting knife." I let go of another string. "But how fortunate he was," I said, pulling both my hands apart and drawing the strings taut, "for he had not dropped his sturdy hunting spear." Her tiny mouth made the shape of an O when I showed her the spear I had made with the string. She smiled when I was finished.

"You must try and sleep now," I told her.

Steps Softly snuggled deeper under the covers and held out her hand. "I'm staying right here with you," I reassured her. Apoppa and Tiintuk nestled by each of her arms. I took off my caribou jacket and draped it on top of us. I crawled under the covers, too, and held my sister's hand.

"Close your eyes now, we must rest." I whispered a song for us: "Night sky watching over me, the dark beginning of time. Shooting stars, to brighten a path. For children of the northern lights." Sensing from her gentle, even breathing that Steps Softly was slowly falling asleep, I turned my head toward the ceiling and let myself relax for the first time that day.

Many thoughts filled my mind. The fury of the polar bear. The loss of Grandmother. The catch of fish sacrificed to the bear. The deep ache I held in my chest for Mother and Father. I stroked my baby sister's hand and smoothed a strand of shining black hair on her forehead. Sleep, little one, I heard myself say. Sleep, little one. I will care for you. My mind struggled to think of plans for the morning. Where would we go? What would we eat? Should I try and find Mother and Father? But the wind howling and the shrill rasp and hiss of the driving snow were my lullaby toward a dreamless night of chilling sleep.

Mrs. TenBroeck closed the book.

"Uuuhhhh-uuuuummm," Mrs. Dildine said, clearing her throat and standing behind everyone. The students jumped.

"Line up for gym," Mrs. TenBroeck said.

"And Miss Stritch, I'd like to talk to you," Mrs. Dildine added.

Everyone but Harper stood by the door.

"It's about my immunization records, isn't it?" Harper said, walking alongside Mrs. Dildine.

"Yes, it is."

"Well, I'll tell my mother."

"Technically . . ." Mrs. Dildine started to say.

"I know," Harper interrupted, "I'm not even supposed to be in school without them. Believe me, this isn't the first time I've heard this."

"Start on down to the gym. AND WALK!" Mrs.

Dildine ordered. She gave Harper a strange look, but Harper didn't even notice.

After gym, Mrs. TenBroeck stood behind her desk and pulled out a shoe box which she held high in the air. She leaned over to close the bottom drawer of her desk as she spoke. "I realize that this may only look like an ordinary shoe box to you."

"No duh," Stephanie Grissom muttered.

Mrs. TenBroeck whirled around, taking off her glasses and glaring at a number of students. "Who said that?" she demanded.

There was absolute silence. She slowly returned her glasses to the middle of her nose.

"As I was saying, remember to bring one in tomorrow," she began again. "This may only look like an ordinary shoe box, but by tomorrow afternoon when we've finished, you will find yourselves the proud owners of a class A, number one, bo-na-fide depository at your desks for your very own valentines. It's been a standard practice of mine to have a valentine party in my room." Mrs. TenBroeck hesitated and took off her glasses. "Provided everyone behaves and gets his or her work done." She tapped her plan book, walking down the middle aisle. "We're also going to have a Cupid's Sweetheart Contest Bulletin Board. Remember to bring in one of your baby pictures and make sure you don't show it to anyone."

"What kind of baby picture?" asked Harold Pon.

"Any picture of you as a little kid," Mrs. TenBroeck explained. She pointed to one of the side bulletin boards. "I'll put them up there, and you're going to try and guess which sixth grader is which baby."

Melody Briscoe suddenly turned to Harold. "Did you look Chinese when you were a baby?" she asked.

Harold squinted at her in amazement. "No, Melody," he said in disbelief, "I looked like Daffy Duck when I was a baby." Harold put his head down on his desk and pounded his fist on the top several times.

As luck would have it, Miss Natalie had one of her headaches so that YL and Sophie could go right up to Harper's apartment before heading home. They didn't have far to go to find her, since she was sitting on the landing waiting for them. They could hardly believe what she told them. Even Harper was struggling to make sense of what her mother had admitted.

"It still hasn't sunk in yet," Harper explained. "I keep saying it over and over again. My father IS NOT dead. My mother and father are only divorced."

"Your father isn't dead?" YL repeated.

"I don't understand," Sophie said.

"My father is alive," Harper answered. "My mother always let me believe that my father was dead, but when I came home last night, I told her I couldn't find his name listed on The Wall. I said I wanted to know what was going on. I asked her to explain it to me."

Harper hesitated. "I can't figure out, though, why she lied to me."

"Maybe she stretched the truth," YL told Harper.

Harper's face flushed with anger. "She let me believe all these years that my father was dead. I call that more than *stretching* the truth."

"Maybe your mom didn't know what to tell you," Sophie offered. "Maybe she thought it was easier than explaining that she'd divorced your dad."

"Maybe she wasn't sure how to explain what happened," YL added.

"You both sound like my mother." Harper got up and stomped into her apartment. "Whose side are you on, anyway?" She walked across the living room floor and plopped down on the couch. YL and Sophie followed her.

YL sat down next to Harper and said, "We're not on anyone's side."

Harper looked at YL. "My mother lied about the whole thing. She admitted it last night."

"What did she say?" YL asked.

"She told me that she didn't think I needed to *know* my father. That right before they got divorced, he acted very strange." Harper slammed her fist into the pillow of her lap. "She said that after he came home from Vietnam, he was different. She said she thought he wasn't the same man. He even spent time getting counseling."

"Was that why she divorced him?" Sophie questioned.

"Mom said she got scared. She told me she'd wake up at night and find him stalking around the apartment with an M-16, convinced the place was surrounded by VC."

"M-16? VC?"

"An M-16's a rifle. VC are Vietcong."

"Was it true? I mean, was your apartment surrounded by VC?"

"No," Harper said with disbelief. "Sophie, VC are soldiers in Vietnam. We lived in Tacoma, Washington, at the time."

"Do you think being in the war made him do strange things?"

"According to what mom said."

"Enough for her to take you away? Maybe she was afraid for your safety," YL suggested.

"I guess so."

Sophie picked up Jupiter, cradled her like a baby, and rubbed her stomach. "But didn't you have relatives looking for you? Didn't your mother have parents? Brothers? Uncles?"

"It's almost like you were able to fade away into the woodwork," YL said.

"She always told me I didn't have any living grandparents—at least not on her side of the family. She said my dad became a stranger, and when he stopped going to his counseling sessions, she got so nervous that one day, when he left to go to work, she packed whatever clothes would fit into one suitcase, picked me up, and simply walked out the door." Harper stood up and paced back and forth. "Mom said she filed for divorce after Dad was sent to Germany, and it was granted." Harper sat down again.

"Didn't your father ever try to find you? I mean, I can't imagine my dad not looking for me," YL said.

"Nope," Harper answered. "At least, I guess not. But now that I think about it . . ." She stopped, mid-sentence. Harper's face was returning to its naturally light-pink color. She leaned back on the sofa, clutching a pillow. "Holy cow, all I've been thinking about is how angry I am that I've got a father somewhere that I didn't know about. But my dad's known about me all along. Maybe *he's* been looking for *me!*" She closed her eyes for a second, but sat bold upright. She snapped her fingers loudly. "Maybe that's why I don't have any school records. Maybe that's why I've had every school nurse across the country asking me about my shots and immunization records." Harper stood up. "Maybe we've been on the run," she said, her face suddenly brightening.

"What do you mean?" Sophie asked.

"I mean, every time we start to get settled in a new place, and I start to make friends and my mom gets a good job, wham, all of a sudden, out of a clear blue sky, we up and move." Harper tossed the pillow on the couch. "What if it's because my father is getting too close? What if we've moved because he's almost found us? Maybe he traced our address or, better yet, our phone number. I don't know." She sat down again, her face having lost its excited expression. "I mean, how *would* I know? I always went wherever my mom took me."

Sophie looked stunned.

YL stood up. He paced in front of the couch. "You don't suppose, Harper, that your name is different, too? I mean, I saw a story on TV about this father in New Hampshire who stole his own kids and changed their names. In the beginning they were Phillip, Kirsten, and Sarah, but by the time they got to Montana, their names were Jerry, Sherry, and Donna. How would you have known if your mom changed your name? You were only a little kid."

Harper looked thoughtful. "That's possible, isn't it?" she said, covering her face with the pillow then placing it in her lap. "What if I'm not even Harper Lee Stritch, after all?"

"How could you find out?" Sophie questioned.

"Where's your birth certificate?" YL asked. "Every little kid has a birth certificate or a baby book."

"I don't know what to think. Mom said she couldn't find the certificate when I asked her about it."

YL patted Jupiter on the head. "Do you remember anything about your father at all?" he asked.

"Sometimes," she answered quietly, "I think I can almost remember his face." She stared past Sophie and YL. "Parts of his face, stuff like a man's face that was very shiny and hot and smooth." She touched the side of her cheek. "There was this kind of smell about him, too. Not a bad smell, but an aftershave kind of smell. One time I was in a men's store, and I thought of my father. I was near a counter that had men's cologne. I remember thinking of him because of that smell." Harper looked at YL and Sophie as she spoke. "And for some reason, I think of him as being *very big*, so big that when I held my hand up against his palm, my hand was completely lost. And I remember his laugh, this big, kind of booming laugh. I hope he's better now. I hope he's a nice person."

"I'm *sure* your father is a nice person," Sophie said, trying to sound reassuring.

"All little kids think their parents are big," YL offered. "That's what my dad says, anyway."

Honk! Honk! Evan had arrived for Sophie. YL looked out the window and saw his dad's car pulling into a parking space.

Sophie stood up, handing Jupiter to Harper. "What are you going to do?"

"I don't know for sure," Harper answered. "Here I thought my father was dead all this time. And now I find out I've got a father that my mother doesn't want me to know. Or see."

YL and Sophie looked at each other.

"And you know the worst part of all this?" Harper added.

Sophie grabbed her dance bag. YL put one arm through his backpack.

"What?" they asked in unison, forgetting to say jinx.

"It's all so confusing. My dad's dead, then he's alive. Then Mom tells me she thinks I'd be better off if I didn't get to know him. *But,* maybe he's looking for me. Maybe that's why we keep moving around the country for no good reason." Harper looked directly at Sophie.

The deep blasts of a fire truck making a run in front of Harper's apartment muffled Evan's honking.

Harper sank back into the couch. "This is one big mess." She rolled her eyes. "Maybe my name is really Bertha Foofnaggle. Or Hortense Pantyhose."

Sophie and YL didn't know whether to laugh or cry. The blasts of the fire engine grew louder and louder.

YL put his hand on Harper's shoulder. "Everything's going to get straightened out. I'm sure it will. When my parents got divorced, it was like World War Three, but they can even talk to each other now. They can actually be in the same room together." YL made a face. "Well, sometimes."

Sophie and YL started toward the door.

"Can you come over Friday night?" asked Sophie.

"I guess," Harper answered.

"We could build our dioramas. You could spend the night. YL's going to be there."

"Don't go bananas on us," YL teased. "You're the brains behind our igloo. We need you," he said with a grin. Harper gave him a good-natured punch in the arm.

Evan honked again. Sophie and YL vanished around the corner and down the stairs.

Harper stood at the window with Jupiter in her arms. She watched the bright, red taillights of the cars trailing away as Evan and Mr. Truax drove off.

Looking down at Jupiter, Harper asked, "Who am I?" The cat purred and purred as Harper rubbed Jupiter's stomach. "Jupiter, you wouldn't care if I were Prunella Puddingcake as long as you got fed, would you?" Jupiter closed her eyes and proceeded to fall asleep. "That's what I thought," Harper said.

Harper looked out at the night sky and spotted the planet Venus, twinkling brightly in spite of the city lights. As she scratched Jupiter under the chin, the cat leaned her head back to give Harper more neck to rub. "What do you say, Jupe? Everyone seems to know who I am but me." Jupiter closed her eyes again. While the cat snoozed, Harper picked up her magic eight ball which was on top of the bookshelf and flipped it over so that it would give her a new reading. "What do you say, magic eight ball? Since my father can't find *me*, should I try and find *him*?" She tipped it and waited so that the whitish triangle holding the answer showed up in the blue water. Finally, as the water cleared, Harper read aloud, *"Signs Point to Yes."*

"That settles it," Harper said, half talking to herself, half talking to Jupiter. She carried her cat over to the stand with the telephone. Harper opened up the phone book to the front section listing long-distance area codes. Jupiter hopped onto the tabletop, walking in circles beside the telephone.

"Tacoma, Tacoma," Harper mumbled. "Tacoma, Washington," she said aloud as she ran her finger down the list of states and column of three-digit numbers. "That's the last place my father lived and the first place I'll try. Area code two-oh-six." She dialed the number for Information. Jupiter purred and purred and rubbed up against her arm.

"Hello? Information? Do you have a phone number listed for a Mr. Ronald Lee Stritch?"

CHAPTER SIXTEEN

A Bowling Ball, a Broncobuster, and a Pixie

"**M**om, there's not one baby picture here I'd want to take into school," Sophie said as the two of them sorted through a shoe box full of old family photographs. Evan stood behind the counter, eavesdropping.

"You *were* a wee bit plump when you were little," her mother commented.

"Let's face it, Mom, I was downright fat," Sophie admitted, staring at one picture. "I looked like a bowling ball with little stubby legs and arms."

"Yes, but it was convenient," Evan joked, "whenever we wanted to take you somewhere, we just rolled you down the sidewalk."

"Not funny," Sophie replied with a frown.

"I prefer to think of you as plump," Mrs. Spagnolo commented, holding up another picture in which Sophie wore a frilly dress and a bow in her hair. "Why don't you let me find a picture?"

Sophie couldn't tell if her mother was teasing or serious. Her father came in from fixing the dripping sink in Room 9. When he heard what Sophie needed, he opened his wallet.

"Now this one," he said, taking a picture out of its plastic casing, "is my favorite. I show this one whenever anyone asks to see a picture of my kids."

Sophie looked at the dog-eared photo. "Oh, Dad, how could you?" she moaned when she saw an image of a grinning, toothless toddler.

"I'm just glad they're not holding a Cupid's Contest like that at the high school," Evan said. "The only pictures of me anyone would find are from my geek phase which lasted about ten years."

"And who says you're out of your geek phase now?" Sophie returned.

"Very humorous, punkin face," Evan replied. "Don't forget, I can always tell family secrets about you to your friends when they come over tomorrow night." He leaned over Sophie's shoulder and took a look at the picture her father had given her. "This one's actually kind of cute."

"Okay, I'll take it," Sophie said. "And just as soon as the Cupid's Contest is over, I'm going to burn it, Dad."

"Over my dead body," her father said, trying to snatch it back.

"Did you and Mom ever want to have more kids than just me?" YL asked his father as they went through one of the moving boxes looking for a baby picture.

His father made an "I'm concentrating" face. "Yes and no," he answered.

"Does that mean yes, you did, or no, you didn't?"

"A little of both. Here," Dwayne Truax said, handing his son several envelopes, "you look through these." He kept several for himself. "I think we took all of these pictures in Cheyenne during the last two years." He dug deeper in the box. "What we need are the pictures from Detroit."

YL carefully stacked each photo after he looked at it.

"Now if it were up to me," his father said, "I'd find the picture I took of you naked in the bathtub."

"Right, Dad." YL frowned. "Did you and Mom want to have a girl or a boy?"

His father looked at him suspiciously.

"Actually, we talked about getting a puppy, but we never did. Besides, you were a lot cuter than a puppy."

"No, seriously, Dad."

"I am being serious," his father replied. "All we wanted was a healthy kid. Girl or boy didn't matter."

YL held up a photo of his mother holding him as he struggled to take his first baby steps. "How about this one?"

YL's father shook his head. "Don't you want a picture with only you in it?"

"I like this picture with Mom in it." YL hesitated. "What would you do, Dad, if Mom got married again?"

"Why do you ask? Do you know something I don't?"

"Maybe."

"Is the guy's name Phillip?"

YL's eyes popped open. "How did you know?"

"I'm not as dense as you think."

"Oh."

"Well? Don't leave me in suspense. Did she call and announce the other night that she was getting married?"

YL nodded.

"How come you didn't tell me?"

"I thought it would make you mad. She even wants me to go out there over spring vacation to meet him. He has two daughters." YL made a face.

His father didn't answer, but picked up another stack of pictures and sorted through them.

"Dad, what will you do when she gets married again?"

His father looked up and raised his eyebrows. "Be glad for her, I guess."

YL felt relieved. He came across a picture he remembered well. "Hey, how about this one?" The photograph showed a little boy wearing pajamas plus a cowboy hat and boots, riding on a rock-'em, sock-'em plastic rocking horse.

His father took the picture and studied it. "Now that's one of my favorites. YL, the broncobuster. I think you should take this one."

"It's not going to be much of a contest, though, trying to identify Carnell and me," YL explained.

"Why's that?"

"Easy, he and I are the only black kids in the room."

*   *   *

Harper sat at the kitchen table, her left palm held in front of her face, her right hand holding *Palm and Fingerprint Reading Made Easy*. Jupiter watched from the kitchen counter.

As Harper mumbled to herself, her face had a puzzled look. "Does your Life line encircle the Mount of Venus?" she read from the book. She studied her palm again. "What Mount of Venus?" she asked, and flipped to the back of the book to find an explanation. "Okay, it's the fleshy lump at the base of my thumb," she explained aloud after looking in the Palmistry glossary. She returned to the basic instruction section. Gazing steadily at her Life line, she tried to read from the book. "A Life line encircling the Mount of Venus with a Head line moving directly toward the root of the thumb means conflict. A rocky road lies ahead." Harper squinted at the tiny lines. "Holy cow," she whispered, "my Head line crashes into my Life line." Jupiter, having lost interest in watching Harper, licked a paw and washed an ear.

Harper's mother came in the door. "Hey, sport, how come you're still up?"

Harper continued to study her hand. "I'm figuring out my Heart line."

Caroline Stritch put her backpack by the closet, pulled out a chair, and sat down next to her daughter. "Why don't you let me have a look at your hand?" She held it gently and gave it a kiss.

"Mom, you're supposed to read my palm. Not kiss my hand."

"Okay. Okay. I got carried away." Harper's mother swirled her hands in the air and closed her eyes. "Summon my powers, oh, crystal ball." She opened one eye and sneaked a peak at Harper. "The great Caroline will now read your palm. Oh . . ."

"Mom, you don't have a crystal ball," Harper said, rolling her eyes.

Caroline Stritch drew her index finger down the center of Harper's palm.

"I see a long life," her mother predicted, showing Harper how her Life line began on the middle edge of her palm and extended to her wrist. "And a strong Head line, crossing into your Life line." Her mother looked up. "A sure sign of stubbornness, but we already know that!"

Harper grinned.

"And look at this," her mother added, "a wide gap between your Head line and Life line suggests daring. Maybe even recklessness!"

"What does it say about my love life?"

"What love life, you're only twelve years old!"

"Moooom!"

Caroline Stritch held her daughter's palm close to her face. "Mmmmmm," she muttered, "very interesting," she commented. "I see a very deep Heart line, which means that you have a great deal of passion in you. But names of secret admirers, the great Caroline cannot predict. It's much too soon."

Harper giggled.

"To end my reading," her mother said with a flourish, "I, by your Sun line, see that you will be taking a long trip."

Harper eagerly sat up. "Where?" she asked.

"Oh, I was only joking," her mother replied. "Palm readers always say that. It's a standard line. You will be taking a long trip." Her mother suddenly grew very serious.

"See this line?" she asked, holding out her own hand.

Harper looked carefully as her mother pointed to her own palm.

"Yes."

"This is my mistake line."

Harper looked at her hand, searching for a mistake line. "I don't see mine. Do I have one? Was that in the book?"

"No, no, honey," her mother explained, "only adults get one of these."

Harper looked up.

"This mistake line on my hand, Harper, is there for a reason. I've made some real goofs in my life. Not telling you about your father was one."

Harper watched as her mother worked at finding the right words to say. She interrupted: "Was I a mistake, Mom?"

"No, sweetie, you weren't a mistake," she explained. Then she smiled. "You were a little bit of a surprise, but no mistake. That's for sure.

"When all of the things with your father were going on, Harp, I thought I was doing the right thing. I thought we'd get a chance to start over, fresh. I hope you can believe me on that. I thought at the time that I was doing the right thing. Only telling a lie like that wasn't really the right thing. Lies always catch up with you. Believe me, I've found out the hard way."

Harper kept still. Her mother reached across the table and took both of her hands. "Are you still mad at me about your father, Harp? Can you find it in your heart to forgive me? I started a lie by telling you that he was dead. Doing that was a terrible mistake. I didn't know how to get out of it, so the best I could do was keep it going," her mother confessed.

Harper nodded. "All I want to do, Mom, is find out who my father is," she said innocently. "I just want to know what he's like. How he talks. If he likes fried chicken or not."

Caroline Stritch held her daughter's right hand in both of hers, then drew it up to her face. She took a deep breath.

"I've thought about this all day," she said. "In some ways, I've known this was coming, but I always dreaded it."

Harper watched her mother.

"If you can just give me some time, I think I can come to terms with what it's going to take to put you in touch with your father." She watched her daughter carefully.

"Why's it so hard to call him? Do you hate each other that much?"

"No, it isn't anything like that. It's just that," Harper's mother explained hesitatingly, "you're the only thing I have, and I've always been so afraid of losing you the way I lost my parents."

Harper stood up and gave her mother a hug.

"Maybe in a few weeks," Caroline Stritch continued, "I'll try and find out how to contact him. Maybe we could even call him and you could talk to him on the phone."

"Really?"

"Really. I promise. Next week is midterms and I'm going to be going a little crazy with those, but . . ." Harper's mother shifted in her chair. Harper stood up and let her mother's arms surround her.

"Do we have to wait so long?" Harper asked.

"I need a little time on this, Harp," she said, getting up and unzipping a pocket on her backpack. "Here." She handed her daughter a small photograph. "I found this last night after you went to bed."

Harper stared at the picture of the child. Her mother looked over her shoulder.

"What a little pixie you were when you were a baby," Caroline Stritch commented. "You were always into some kind of mischief."

"Thanks for the picture, Mom," Harper said, giving her mother a hug.

"I couldn't have you be the only kid in class without a photograph to put up on the bulletin board."

Rather than say anything else, Harper simply hugged her mother again, but this time she hugged her with one enormous hug, as big and as long a hug as Harper could ever remember.

CHAPTER SEVENTEEN

Pasghetti

While the students in Room 17 had TNT and listened to Beethoven's Seventh Symphony in A Major, Opus 92, Mrs. TenBroeck thumbtacked baby pictures to the bulletin board. Red hearts and cupid silhouettes graced both corners. White lace doilies served as frames with baby pictures Scotch-taped in their centers. Mrs. TenBroeck kept stepping back from the board to survey her work.

She assembled the pictures into a giant heart shape and placed a large, heart-shaped list of the student's names in the middle. Pieces of red yarn were attached to each picture. On Valentine's Day, the student who correctly identified all the photos would receive a special prize, then the strings would connect each name with each photograph.

Mrs. TenBroeck asked Loren and Harold to clear off the reading tables. "We'll put the dioramas there for Parents' Night," she explained. "And the cinquains you wrote will hang on this bulletin board," she said, pointing to the empty expanse of wall beside Rayna. "I want your parents to see some of the work you've been doing in this room. Now, if you'll clear off your desks, we have enough time for a chapter from the story before lunch." Mrs. TenBroeck looked over her bifocals. "Matter-of-fact, why don't you get yourself settled in with paper and scissors and start cutting out the designs for your valentine boxes while I read?"

Earlier in the day, every shoe box in the room had been covered in white butcher paper and a slot had been cut into the tops. The only thing left for the students to do was the exterior decorations. Sophie took out crayons, glue, and scissors. Steve Coffinburger distributed bands of red crepe paper.

"Everyone set?" Mrs. TenBroeck asked, looking over the top of the book.

A few students drew and snipped, coloring various spots on the boxes here and there, looking up occasionally, while others lettered their names across the sides. Several students sat very still and simply listened as Mrs. TenBroeck began to read.

Chapter Six: For two days and nights, the drifter howled around us. Steps Softly and I remained huddled under blankets trying to conserve what little energy we had. Even the puppies seemed to understand the importance of saving their strength. The blinding snow kept me from hunting for food or even trying to venture outside to identify land markings. Several

times, I thought of returning to our old igloo for sup-
plies, but I knew I would be breaking tradition to enter
a dwelling where someone had died, and so I resigned
myself to staying where we were and using what I had
brought along.

I felt so helpless watching Steps Softly as she slowly
grew weaker and weaker from lack of food. I encouraged her to sleep, hoping her small body could store
enough energy in case we might need to set out to find
Mother and Father. I allowed myself to use one match
each day for lighting our soapstone lamp. I melted ice
so that we would have water to drink.

How would I find food for us? How would I find
Mother and Father? These were my gravest concerns.
Should I set out with my baby sister to search for our
parents? Or should we stay where we were? During the
times Steps Softly rested, I battled these thoughts one
against the other like two bachelor walrus fighting
along the shoreline.

When Steps Softly was awake, I played small games
with her from the tiny box of toys I'd brought along.
Toys I had long ago outgrown. I told string stories I
knew of Sedna, the goddess of the seas, and the tale of
a giant and his crumbing icehouse. Using my knife, I
drew first one tale into the snow, then wiping away
that story, I drew another. But I could tell from the
weary expression on Steps Softly's face that she grew
weaker and weaker with each passing hour.

As day edged slowly toward night, I took her hand
in mine and told her that I would tell her only one
more tale, then she must try and sleep. Her shining
eyes had lost their sparkle, but she nodded. It was

then, at that moment, that I realized we would have to try and move on, for the chances of Father and Mother or anyone finding us were growing dimmer and dimmer. While I gathered my thoughts surrounding the stories Grandmother had told me many times, I was also thinking of the best way for us to travel. What should I take? In what direction should I set off? And what, if any, food would I be able to find?

With those questions weighing heavily on my mind, I began the telling of a spirit tale. Once, I whispered to Steps Softly, there was a mighty hunter who kept losing the meat he tried to store away for the long winter days. Each day after hunting, he stored the meat he had caught in a secret cache in a nearby cave. But by the next morning, his store of meat was always gone. This angered the hunter. He vowed to get revenge on the person who was stealing it. To discover the thief, the hunter hid himself in the very back of the cave, staying there two, even three, days without leaving.

Finally, the weary hunter saw a group of children appear magically out of a shimmering mist. These children gathered around the meat and began to eat heartily. The hunter leaped out from behind a boulder to attack the children. As he did so, they became transparent, and the thrusts of his spear never touched them. Their voices echoed throughout the cave and became so loud that the noise roared in his head. He dropped his spear to cover his ears with his hands. The hunter realized that the children were spirit children, the children of the northern lights, who had come down from the starlit heavens. Once the children had calmed the mighty hunter, they explained that they had been having a season of hunger, a season of severe famine. This starvation had caused the lack of shimmering northern lights. Wouldn't the hunter please share his store of meat with the children? they begged. If he did this, they promised the northern lights would return to the skies to shimmer and entertain him once more. The hunter considered this carefully, and in the end, he relented. "Take what you want of my cache of meat," he offered.

Several nights later, the hunter was standing alone on a barren hill when the northern lights began to glimmer and shine all across the sky from one end of the horizon to the other. The hunter smiled and waved his arms in recognition. "Aiyee, aiyee!" he shouted. As he did this, he was very pleased because of a sound he heard that filled the skies and stretched across the endless landscape. A joyous sound. He heard the laughter of little children.

By the end of my story Steps Softly was asleep. I placed my arms around her. I suddenly longed to see the faces of my mother and father. I longed to hear one of my mother's songs. She often sang to us each evening as we fell asleep. And so, I quietly sang that night for myself and my sleeping sister.

Each day, fill me with wonder, bring something new
    my way.
Each evening, send the rising moon, shower the skies
    with stars from the heavens.
Darkest of nights, invite the faithful moon,
    changing from full to crescent.

Give me strength to search the dawn for morning's
glow and arise to meet a new day dawning.
Arise to see the new light, the new bright light, whitening the morning sky.
Arise to greet a new day with hope.

These words brought me comfort as the wind
howled around us. And in my worried and hungered
state, I fell asleep, not noticing that the drifter had
slowly but surely blown itself out.

As the doors of #128 closed, YL handed Mr. Duke
a note in Dwayne Truax's handwriting.

"So, Mr. Truax, you'll be getting off with my friend,
Sophie, huh?" Mr. Duke said, putting the note into
the pocket of his plaid shirt.

"Yes sir," YL answered, taking a seat next to Sophie.

She poked YL in the ribs and whispered in his ear.
She'd told him about Mr. Duke's jokes, and the two
were ready and waiting to see what Mr. Duke was
going to say. After most of the other riders had gotten
off the bus at their stops, Mr. Duke took off his cap and
smoothed his hair, a sure sign that he was ready to
begin.

"So tell me, Sophie, what do you call a hot and
noisy duck?" he asked.

Sophie thought for a second, but YL answered,
without hesitating, "A firequacker."

Mr. Duke looked into his mirror. "Hmmmm," he

muttered, "I think we've got a live wire here." He maneuvered the bus through a set of detour signs, then began to ask another joke. "All right, Mr. Truax, what's harder to catch the faster you run?"

Again, YL didn't hesitate. "Your breath," he replied.

"Wow," Mr. Duke said. "What do you say, Sophie? Maybe I've met my match."

As the bus pulled up to the motel, Mr. Duke cleared his throat and declared, "Okay, this is a toughie. Are you ready for my one and only Valentine's Day joke?"

YL and Sophie nodded as the bus scraped and screeched to a halt. Mr. Duke flipped out the STOP sign. He checked his side mirrors for cars behind him. "The pressure is on," he admitted with a sly grin. "Tell me, you two, why is it I have so much trouble spelling Cupid?" he asked.

YL stood on the top step, his backpack over his arm, a furrowed line between his eyebrows. Sophie stood right behind him and looked puzzled, too.

"I don't know," Sophie admitted, "tell us."

"Hey," YL stopped her, "don't give up so easy."

A car honked behind the bus.

"Okay, okay, we give up," YL said finally. "Why is it you have so much trouble spelling Cupid, Mr. Duke?"

"Because every time I get to C-U, I forget everything else," Mr. Duke said with a smile.

YL shook his head.

Sophie and YL waved at Mr. Duke from the other side of the highway as the bus pulled away.

"See," Sophie said, "I told you they're always corny but cute."

Harper set the cardboard box with her weighted-down, half-finished igloo by the stairs. She pulled her mother's old bowling ball bag out of the closet and began calling Jupiter's name.

"Are you sure the Spagnolos don't mind if you bring Jupiter?" Harper's mother questioned.

"I'm sure it's going to be fine," Harper said, her fingers crossed behind her back. "Besides, we couldn't leave Jupiter alone in the apartment tonight," she added. "I'll be at Sophie's house. You're going to stay overnight at Buckhannon with the basketball team. Jupiter would be alone."

Caroline Stritch picked up her bags and the igloo box. She started down the stairs. "Don't forget your toothbrush," she called out. "Pull the door shut. I've got the house keys with me."

"Okay," Harper replied. She'd already packed her backpack with pajamas, toothbrush, comb, and clean clothes for the next day. She looked through the apartment one last time. She took her mother's bowling ball out of the bag and set the ball on the sofa.

Harper tucked a can of cat food into the side pocket where the bowling shoes were normally placed, and pulled a chair over to the hallway closet. She reached into the box on the top shelf, felt inside for the old soft, green blanket and gave a tug.

"Harper," her mother called from downstairs, "hurry up. We've got to get a move on."

"I'll be right there," Harper answered, giving another yank. Out popped the blanket, *and* a book tumbled to the floor. Jupiter curiously sniffed a corner of the cover. Harper turned it over.

Baby's First Five Years.

"Holy moley," she said, "look what I found." She quickly tucked the book into her backpack beside her pajamas and toothbrush.

"Come on, Jupiter," she coaxed. "You're going on a little adventure," she explained, picking up the cat. Jupiter spread all four legs apart when Harper tried to put the cat into the bowling-ball bag. "Aw, come on, Jupe, give me a break," she pleaded. Harper stuffed Jupiter's head down as she zippered the bag, leaving a small breathing hole on the side.

Jupiter's pink nose and a whisker or two popped out of the opening. The cat gave a tiny, muffled meow.

"You wouldn't believe what I just found," Harper told Sophie and YL, setting her things on Sophie's bed. "Look at this," Harper said, pulling the baby book from her backpack. Sophie stared at the butterflies and bunnies on the cover of *Baby's First Five Years*. Harper seated herself on the edge of the bed and began turning pages. She flipped through the book. "Just look at all these pictures of me." She quickly stopped, holding one picture close to her face. "Oh, my gosh, this must be my dad!" she exclaimed, her finger pointing to a tall, broad-shouldered man with a head full of wavy black hair. She looked up at Harper and YL. "This must be my father!" She smiled.

Sophie, YL, and Harper stared at the baby picture and looked at the rounded writing of Harper's mother on labels for first tooth and first words.

A sound came from the bowling bag.

Sophie looked up. "What was that?"

Harper turned her head to listen. "I don't know. Did you hear something?"

YL lifted the bag. "I think this is the answer," he explained.

"Jupiter?" Sophie whispered.

"Holy moley, I forgot," Harper said. She quickly unzipped the bag, and Jupiter's head popped up.

"Meeeeow," she cried.

"How could you bring Jupiter!" Sophie said, turning to Harper. "What are we going to do? My dad's allergic to cats!"

Harper shrugged.

"Kids," Mrs. Spagnolo called from the kitchen, "time for dinner."

Harper took Jupiter out of the bag.

Sophie opened her closet. "Let's hide her in here."

YL made a nest for the cat, using a sweater and pants on the floor.

"You be a good girl," Harper said, patting Jupiter on

the head. Sophie carefully closed the closet door. The three kids tiptoed out of the room, hoping Jupiter would be quiet during dinner.

Sophie led the way to the dining room as Evan handed out plates, knives, forks, spoons, and napkins for everyone to set the table. Lana stood in a corner and watched as YL folded napkins beside each place setting.

"It's pasghetti night," Lana announced. Mrs. Spagnolo brought in a big pot of sauce and positioned it in the middle of the table. Evan set down a basket of garlic bread while Mr. Spagnolo placed small, green salads beside each place.

As he did so, his face began to pucker. At first it was a small twitch that started with his eyes, then waved across his nose. But by the time he'd set all seven salad bowls onto the table, his entire face was contorted. His eyes were beginning to water. His nostrils were flared. His cheeks were splotched with patches of red. As he reached across the table to shake Harper's hand and formally introduce himself, the only thing that came out of his mouth was a loud and raucous "ACHOO" that nearly blew all the napkins off the table.

CHAPTER EIGHTEEN

Ronald Eugene?
Rhonda Jean?

Seated at the Spagnolos' kitchen table, YL stacked sugar cubes on a new igloo while Sophie squirted glue, and Jupiter slept in her closet after a meatball snack. Harper surveyed her earlier attempt at building an igloo.

"I didn't have any luck getting the roof to arch," she commented. "I even stuffed newspaper inside and weighted down the sugar cubes with a couple of books, but . . ." she said, frowning, "it didn't work."

"Don't you think marshmallows would hold up a little better?" Sophie kept asking.

"Don't sit there and gripe at us, Sophie," YL said. "If you think they'd work better, then try them." Sophie began to work on her own igloo of mini marshmallows, but the results were disastrous. The little white blobs slid around in the puddles of glue, and when YL accidentally bumped the table, one whole side caved in. Nothing seemed to be working. Sophie popped a handful of marshmallows into her mouth.

The three igloo builders stared at their creations. Walls sagged. Not one roof was holding across its arch, and none of the igloos resembled anything like the models of the Inuit snow villages they'd seen at the museum.

"A pretty sorry-looking sight, if you ask me," Evan commented on his way out the door to go to the movies. "I'll be home by midnight," he told his mother.

"Well, nobody asked," Sophie replied.

Mr. Spagnolo came into the kitchen, a box of tissues in his hand.

"Need a little engineering assistance?" he asked in between bouts of blowing his nose.

"Anything would be a help," Harper said. "We're not doing too well."

Sophie's mother joined them at the table. "Is the allergy medicine working?" she asked her husband.

Mr. Spagnolo answered with a smile and the blink of a watery eye.

Mrs. Spagnolo surveyed the igloos. "Maybe what's needed here is a little frosting," she offered, going into the kitchen and returning with a bowl of white fluff.

YL and Mrs. Spagnolo worked on the sugar-cube igloo, restacking each block with a dab of frosting. Harper, Sophie, and Mr. Spagnolo began assembling a marshmallow igloo using toothpicks as stabilizers.

"How about shaving cream?" Sophie questioned.

"Nope, it will evaporate," Mr. Spagnolo explained. "It looks great, but it turns to air."

Mrs. Spagnolo watched Harper, YL, and Sophie as they worked. She looked at her husband, then asked, "How are things going in sixth grade these days?"

Harper was the first to answer. "Not bad," she said. "This sixth grade is better than my last sixth grade."

"Yeah, I like this one fine," YL added. "At least we don't have to do calisthenics every morning like we did in my old room."

"Calisthenics?" Harper asked.

"Yeah, Mr. Butler, my old sixth-grade teacher, made us do calisthenics every morning." YL demonstrated—"Ready! Steady! Go!"—jumping up, spreading his legs apart, and clapping his hands at the same time. "One. Two. One. Two."

"Does your teacher ever yell at you?" Mrs. Spagnolo asked.

"Nope," Sophie answered. "Mrs. TenBroeck says she doesn't yell."

"She says she uses a 'supportive tone,'" YL explained.

"Oh, so it's called supportive tone these days," Mrs. Spagnolo said with a laugh.

Mr. Spagnolo looked at Harper and Sophie's marshmallow creation while he licked his fingers. "That's a little more stable," he commented. Their igloo was ready to have the small entry attached to one side. "I have an idea," he said. He left the room, but returned quickly, setting a can of hair spray on the table. Harper and Sophie had fit the entrance onto the main section of the igloo and secured it with icing.

"Are you willing to try one of my lunatic ideas?" he asked.

Harper and Sophie both nodded, saying, "Sure, why not?" at exactly the same time.

"Jinx," YL replied, watching Mr. Spagnolo, who took the can and sprayed the entire igloo and the sections of cardboard covered in aluminum foil. Then he took the flour sifter and dusted confectioners' sugar onto the top. The layer of powdered sugar evened out the sides of marshmallows.

"Hey, it sticks really well," YL said. "Maybe we should try that with ours."

By the time both teams had applied frosting to the aluminum foil and painted small sections of bluish water on pieces of paper to look like ice floes, they were pleased with their work. Still, the sugar-cube igloo was less sturdy looking than the marshmallow creation.

"Maybe this one could be the abandoned igloo that Stars and Steps Softly use?" Harper offered.

Mr. Spagnolo put his face close to the entrance of the igloo. "Hello? Is anyone home?" he asked.

Sophie shook her head. "Sometimes, I don't know about you, Dad."

"That's okay, Sophie. My dad does weird stuff, too," YL replied. "Here," he said, handing her some small gray pebbles, "we can each make an inukshuk."

"What's an inukshuk?" Mr. Spagnolo asked.

"It's a kind of stone monument, like a landmark," Harper explained.

Mr. Spagnolo nodded and continued stabbing marshmallows with toothpicks.

"The only thing left," Sophie said, eyeing their scene, "is to paint the insides of the boxes and set the igloos inside."

"Do you think we could paint the northern lights along the skyline? Where's that picture we had?" YL asked. Sophie used a white, frosting-covered finger to point to the page in the book entitled *The Inuit: Native People of North America.*

She made a street sign by cutting out slips of paper shaped like arrows. On the arrows, she printed Nome, 500 miles. Paris, 6,421 miles, then attached them to a toothpick.

"How about Sydney, 9,578 miles?" Mrs. Spagnolo guessed.

"Sounds good to me," Sophie said, slowly lettering the word Sydney onto a slip of paper.

"How about Whispering Springs?" her father asked, checking a map of the world. "I'd guess it's about 5,339 miles away."

YL took the bottom bunk in Evan's room. Sophie and Harper stayed next door in Sophie's bedroom. Lying in bed that night, Sophie stared at Harper as she pored over the pictures in her baby book. Each photograph seemed to hold a new fascination. Sophie chewed on her left thumbnail. She petted Jupiter, who slept on her chest. Trying not to disturb the cat, Sophie leaned over the bed and grabbed two books from the stack Harper had used to weight down the ceiling of the experimental igloo: *Magical Children* and *To*

Kill a Mockingbird. Sophie leafed through both of them and chose the second one.

She turned to chapter 1 and scanned the pages. The characters were named Scout, Jim, and Atticus. Unexpectedly, a piece of paper fell out of the book. Sophie held it in one hand, and still petting Jupiter, she tried to tuck it into the back of the book. Her fingers touched against a bumpy surface on the paper and she opened it up.

The words across the top were Registry Division, City of Tacoma, Name of Child.

"Harp," Sophie said, sitting up quickly. Jupiter tumbled onto the floor. "Harper, look!" She handed Harper the piece of paper.

"Holy moley," said Harper, studying it.

"It's your birth certificate, isn't it?" Sophie exclaimed.

Harper continued staring. She pointed to a line on the paper and looked up at Sophie. "You're right, Sofe. It's my birth certificate. Can you believe it?"

"What does it say?" Sophie asked, sitting down on the bed beside Harper.

Harper read aloud. "Certificate No. 1341. Sex F, Color W. Name, Maiden Name, and Birthplace of Mother: Caroline Mae Stritch, Monmouth, Oregon. Name, Surname, and Birthplace of Father: Ronald Eugene Lee, Tacoma, Washington. Name of Child." At that part, Sophie stopped. She stared at the line of print.

"Name of Child," Harper read aloud, "Rhonda Jean Lee."

"Rhonda Jean?" Sophie asked in disbelief. "You're really Rhonda Jean Lee!" Sophie studied Harper for a second. "You don't look like a Rhonda."

Harper scooted to the edge of the bed so that her legs hung over the side. "But I am, Sofe," Harper replied. "Remember when you and I were sitting on the couch and YL said, 'You know, Harper, maybe your name is something different.' Geez louise, he was right. My name is really Rhonda."

Before Sophie could say anything, Harper headed out the bedroom door.

"Come on, I'm going to tell YL," she said.

The two girls scurried next door to Evan's room.

"Wake up, YL, wake up!" Harper said, shaking his shoulder.

"Huh? What?" he asked in a groggy voice, sitting up quickly and clunking his head on one of the bottom bars of the top bunk.

"Wake up and meet Rhonda Jean," Sophie announced, sitting down on the edge of the bunk.

"What?" he repeated, rubbing the spot on his forehead.

"Look what we found," Harper said, waving her newly found birth certificate in front of his face. "I'm Rhonda Jean. I'm Rhonda Jean," Harper explained as though she were practicing.

"Rhonda who?" YL asked.

Harper gazed at her image in the mirror over Evan's dresser. "Of course, that's it," she said, turning around, "I'm named after my father."

Sophie looked skeptical. YL still looked half asleep.

Harper's dangly earrings bounced up and down as she spoke. "When a father's named Ronald, and he wants to name a child after himself, it's easy if the baby's a boy." She climbed onto the top bunk and hung over the edge, staring at YL and Sophie. "Then, the father just names the baby boy Ronald. But if the baby's a girl," Harper asked, "what does he name her?"

Sophie quickly understood. "Rhonda," she finished.

"And the Jean is for my grandmother," Harper explained. She took in a deep breath, then nearly shot straight into the air.

"That's it," she said, jumping up and down on the bed like a trampoline. "That's why the information operator didn't have my father's phone number." She snapped her fingers. "Of course!"

"Of course, what?" YL asked.

Harper leaped off the bed. "When I called and asked Information for my father's number, the lady didn't have it," Harper exclaimed. "What a ditz brain I was. I was asking for the wrong name."

"You weren't a ditz brain, Harper," Sophie offered, "you didn't know the other name."

"His *last* name is Lee. Not his *middle* name." Harper ran out of Evan's room, but quickly returned with a book in her hand. "*To Kill a Mockingbird*," Harper read from the book's spine, "by Harper Lee. That's me, isn't it?" she said. "My mother renamed me after this author, this woman, Harper Lee, who wrote *To Kill a Mockingbird*. Now I get it."

Sophie leaned against one of the bunk-bed supports.

She looked toward the hallway. Two little eyes, a pink button nose, and white whiskers peeked around the doorframe.

"Jupiter," Sophie exclaimed, standing up and thunking her head, "how did you get out?" The cat strolled over to her and curiously sniffed the blankets and the cuffs of YL's striped pajamas.

"Sofe," Harper asked suddenly, "can I use your phone?"

"Why?" Sophie asked, picking up Jupiter.

"Just because!"

"What for?"

"I want to call my dad."

"What for?" YL repeated.

"I want to try and call my dad, now that I know his real name."

Sophie hesitated. She wasn't sure what to say. "I guess so," she answered.

"No wonder my father's name wasn't in the phone book. I was asking for the wrong person. I should've asked for Ronald Lee."

Cuddling Jupiter under one arm, Sophie stood up. "Follow me," she said.

She stuffed Jupiter into the double-sided, front pocket of her sweatshirt. In a pair of Evan's old sweat socks, she led the way down the hall to the motel office and the phone.

CHAPTER NINETEEN

Hello?

Sophie punched a button on the telephone to get an outside line and handed the receiver to Harper who dialed Information. YL stood watch by the doorway to the family's living quarters.

"Information?" Harper said loudly.

"Keep your voice down," Sophie cautioned.

"Do you have a phone number for Ronald Eugene Lee?" Harper asked. "That's right, Ronald Eugene Lee." She paused. "You do?" Her eyes widened. Harper danced back and forth. "Quick, quick, get a pencil," she told Sophie who groped through the middle drawer of the reception desk.

"Here!" she said, shoving a pencil nub at Harper.

"Area code 2-0-6," Harper repeated, "5-5-5-9-4-2-3." She quickly scribbled the number on a Crescent Moon Motel notepad. "Thank you very much." She replaced the receiver.

Sophie, Harper, and YL stared at the number on the paper.

"Now what?" YL asked.

"I dial the number," Harper answered.

"Are you sure you don't want your mom to call him first?" Sophie asked.

"Nope. She's extra busy with midterms and basketball finals."

"Maybe you should wait. What are you going to say?" YL said.

"You got me!" Harper replied, throwing her hands up in the air. "But I don't want to wait. If my father's really been trying to find me, he's been waiting longer than I have!" She twisted a corner of her lavender-striped nightshirt. YL turned when he heard Sophie's mother going into the kitchen, waving at Sophie and Harper, motioning for them to keep quiet.

"Over here," Sophie whispered.

Jupiter poked her head out of the side opening of Sophie's sweatshirt. Sophie quietly opened the door to a closetlike room beside the office where a beige phone sat on a coffee table with a driftwood lamp. "Evan hides in here when he wants to have private conversations with Josie Baskim," Sophie explained, fluttering her eyelashes. She pointed to a spot in the corner. "If you sit right there, on the other side of that wall, you can hear *everything* he says to her!"

"No kidding?" YL asked.

"No kidding!" Sophie confirmed, raising her eyebrows.

Harper looked at the phone and took a deep breath. "Ready?"

Sophie and YL gave Harper the okay sign.

"But don't stay on the phone long because Mom could come in," Sophie cautioned.

Harper dialed, then put her hand over the mouthpiece. "It's ringing," she whispered.

Sophie swallowed hard. YL forgot all about watching for Mrs. Spagnolo. Harper tipped the receiver so Sophie and YL could hear. Their heads clunked as they struggled to listen.

Riiiiiing. Silence. *Riiiiiing*. Silence.

Riiiiiing. Click.

A man's deep and businesslike voice answered. "Hello?"

Sophie and YL watched Harper. No one moved. Harper's tongue felt suddenly thick and furry, as if it were covered with a layer of fuzzy green moss.

"Hello? Anybody there?" the man's voice asked.

Harper's hands were clammy cold.

"Hello," she squeaked.

"Yes?" the man responded. "Is anyone there? Who are you calling?"

Harper tried desperately to make sounds come out of her voice box.

"I say, who are you calling?" the man asked.

Harper spoke, but this time she tried to make her voice come out a little clearer, a little stronger. "I'm calling for Mr. Ronald Eugene Lee."

"This is Ron Lee, what can I do for you?" he answered.

YL made motions for Harper to keep talking. Harper seemed to be struggling with what to say next.

"Is this Ronald *Eugene* Lee?" she repeated.

"Yes, it is. Who is this?"

"Mr. Lee, did you have a little girl?" Harper asked quickly. She stammered a second. "I mean, *do* you have a little girl?"

There was a pause on the other end of the phone.

"Is her birthday on January thirteenth?" Harper quizzed.

"Who is this?" Ronald Eugene Lee asked sternly.

"Mr. Lee, I think maybe . . ." Harper started to say, but from out of nowhere, the other phone in the motel office began to ring. Harper stopped speaking. Sophie's heart began to pound. YL stepped over to the doorway and saw Mrs. Spagnolo walk to the reception desk. Harper, Sophie, and YL didn't move a muscle. Mrs. Spagnolo punched a lighted button on the phone.

"Crescent Moon Motel," she said, suddenly coming onto Harper's line. Harper instantly realized Sophie's mom had pressed the wrong button and was connected to the conversation between her and Ronald Eugene Lee in Tacoma, Washington.

"Hang up! Hang up!" Sophie was saying. "Let's get out of here. We'll get into trouble!"

But before Harper had returned the receiver to its beige cradle, she thought she heard the man say something. She wasn't exactly sure what he'd said, though.

"Hurry," Sophie ordered, moving through a side hallway back to the bedroom area. Jupiter poked her head out of Sophie's sweatshirt pocket and meowed loudly.

"In here, in here," YL said, directing Harper toward Sophie's bedroom. He closed the door just in time to hear Mrs. Spagnolo say, "No, I'm sorry, you must have the wrong number."

He leaned his back against the door. "Whew, that was close," he said, looking at Jupiter, but his voice muffled the remaining sentence of Mrs. Spagnolo's conversation.

None of the children heard her when she said, "Yes, sir, I'm positive. There's no one here named Rhonda Jean."

Crystal-like, freezing rain tinged and chinked against the rain gutters outside Sophie's window.

"Do you think that was your dad?" YL asked, scratching Jupiter between her ears.

"Maybe," Harper answered. "It's hard to say. I haven't heard his voice in almost nine years."

"Are you going to try and call again when you get home tomorrow?" Sophie asked.

"That depends," Harper answered.

"On what?" YL asked.

"On whether or not my mother's home," Harper replied.

"Are you going to tell your mother that you tried to call Ronald Eugene Lee in Tacoma?"

"Nope," Harper said quickly. "I think she'd only get mad."

"Maybe it would be better to wait until your mother calls first," YL suggested.

"I suppose so, but . . ." Harper started to say. "Waiting is such a pain-in-the-neck," she remarked.

The freezing droplets began to coat the trees, the roadway, street signs, and bushes, causing everything to sparkle in the light from the orangy Crescent Moon Motel sign.

Harper stood by the window. "Hear that sound?"

"Yep," Sophie answered, yawning and tapping her mouth. She sat up in her bed and propped a pillow behind her back.

"Those are Stars Beyond Counting's tears," Harper said. "I bet they're Stars' tears from crying because she wants to find her parents."

YL rolled his eyes toward the ceiling. "Give me a break," he moaned.

"See," Harper continued, "I think Stars and Steps Softly cry their tears, and by the time the tears get down to earth, they're little crystal raindrops."

"You make it sound like the two girls had died and gone to heaven," YL answered, still shaking his head.

"I bet they're going to be dead, don't you?" Sophie added.

"Naw," Harper replied. "It wouldn't be a very good story for kids if everyone ended up dead."

"True," Sophie said. "Maybe the whole family will get on a plane and go to Disneyland."

"Get serious. Here," YL said, handing Jupiter to Sophie, "I'm going back to bed," he announced. "Harper, did anyone ever tell you that you have a very creative imagination? Good night, you guys." Not waiting for a reply, he went out into the hall.

Jupiter curled herself into a tight ball on Sophie's lap.

"Did you hear that, Jupiter?" Sophie said, kissing the cat's nose. "He called us guys, but we're not guys, are we?"

Jupiter closed her eyes and purred.

Sophie and Harper listened as the sounds of freezing rain continued tinging and pinging against the metal rain gutters. Jupiter and Sophie quickly fell asleep, but Harper lay in bed and stared at the white, flat ceiling and listened to the sounds of the rain for a long, long time.

The only thing not improved by the sheen of ice was the motel sign. For some reason, the freezing rain, or maybe it had been a thin coat of icy water seeping into the old electrical connections, short-circuited an entire set of letters so that the sign only showed

C E E

M   E

CHAPTER TWENTY

Cat Woman, Angel, and Quarterback

Sophie, in her dream, stood next to a carefully trimmed Christmas tree. The entire Spagnolo family sat on the couch in their family room watching her open a stack of presents. Sophie had counted them, thirty-one to be exact, all the same size, the same shape. Every single present was carefully marked DO NOT SHAKE!

"Hurry up," Lana complained. "No one else can open presents until you've finished with yours." Pouting, she crossed her arms and sat on the couch.

"So many presents," Sophie told her parents. "Thank you very, very much." Her parents had robot-like smiles in this dream of hers.

The candy-cane-striped paper tore off easily. Sophie lifted the lid of the box. Out popped a tiny, black-and-white, splotchy-faced kitten.

"Meow, meow," the kitten cried, as if saying, "Feed me! Feed me!"

Sophie cuddled the small ball of fluff. "Oh, thank you. Thank you, Mom! Thank you, Dad! You know I've always wanted a kitten of my own."

Her parents smiled.

"Hurry up," Lana ordered.

As Sophie took another present off the stack, the new kitten climbed onto her lap. The red-and-green-holly-berry wrapping paper pulled off the box on the first try. Sophie removed the lid.

Out popped a tiny, black-and-white, splotchy-faced kitten.

"Meow, meow," the kitten cried, as if saying, "Feed me! Feed me!"

Sophie looked at her parents. She smiled a surprised smile. "Oh, thank you, Mom and Dad. Two kittens will be wonderful."

Her parents smiled.

"Hurry up," Lana repeated.

While Sophie lifted another present from the stack, one kitten clawed its way up the back of Sophie's pajamas. The other kitten tried to perch on Sophie's head.

Sleigh-bell wrapping paper covered the next present and dropped to the floor when Sophie pulled on the first corner. She cautiously peeked under the lid.

Out popped a tiny, black-and-white, splotchy-faced kitten.

Sophie looked at her parents. She tried to smile. "Oh, my goodness, Mom and Dad. Three kittens," she started to say, but was lost for words.

"Meow, meow," the kitten cried, as if saying, "Feed me! Feed me!"

"Hurry up," Lana repeated.

Sophie cautiously lifted another present from the stack. From all different directions, the three kittens simultaneously attacked Sophie's curls that dangled above her shoulders.

The jolly faces of half a dozen rosy-cheeked Santa Clauses covered the wrapping paper on the next package. Sophie hesitated before she pulled at the Scotch tape on the sides. The wrapping paper fell to the floor. One of the kittens playfully pounced on it. This time, Sophie never even got the lid off the box before she heard *Meow! Meow!* as if it were saying, *Feed me! Feed me!*

Sophie looked at her parents, then looked at the remaining stack of boxes. "Mom? Dad?" she mumbled. She lifted the lid.

Out popped a tiny, black-and-white, splotchy-faced kitten.

Pointing toward the other twenty-seven boxes, Sophie tried to speak, but the four kittens climbed up her arms, nibbled on her earlobes, batted at her pierced earrings, and licked her chin.

"Mom? Dad?" Sophie asked. "Are all these boxes filled with kittens?"

Her dream parents had painted, wooden smiles.

"Hurry up," Lana ordered.

"Mom. Dad," Sophie muttered.

Her parents smiled like department-store mannequins. The kitten licking Sophie's chin pushed harder and harder with its raspy tongue. *Scraaatch! Scraaatch!*

"Mom? Dad?" Sophie struggled to say between kitten attacks.

Scraaatch! Scraaatch! Scraaatch!

"Oh, no!" Sophie heard herself say aloud. Then she woke herself up with a start to find Jupiter standing on her chest and licking her chin with long, sandpapery kisses.

"Oh, Jupiter, it's only you," Sophie said, relieved to find only one cat.

Harper's sleep was filled with one dream after another that night at Sophie's house. Every person in her dreams opened his mouth to speak, but each had a strange characteristic: the deep booming voice of a man. Songs and rhymes from childhood played in the background like dinner music at a restaurant. "This is the way the ladies ride, tra-la, tra-la, tra-la. This is the way the cowboys ride, ba-dum, ba-dum, ba-dum."

The little child Harper saw in each of her dreams smiled, giggled, and threw her head back and laughed. Harper saw herself as a little girl, her straight hair pulled into a ponytail, sticking up on top of her head. Peering down from a cloudlike perch like a fluttering angel, Harper watched a much younger version of herself in a frilly lavender dress tightly holding onto a man's hands. "Trot-trot to Boston." The little girl bounced up and down on the man's knee. Up. Down.

Side to side. "Trot-trot to Lynn." Up. Down. Side to side.

Harper, the angel, tried to blink the fuzziness away. Her mouth opened to ask *Is this real? Are you my father? Do you remember me?* The angel struggled to tune in each dream as if she were watching some kind of picture on the television where she could turn a dial to focus the images a little better. She wanted to see everything a little sharper, a little clearer.

Do I remember this man? His eyes? His smooth cheeks? Harper, the angel, asked. But every time the angel flew to another cloud to get a better look, a mist veiled her vision.

There was one thing that never faded away, though. The man's voice. His voice stayed the same.

"My little darlin'," he called out to the lavender-winged angel in the clouds. "My little darlin'."

Every single time that Harper heard this voice, heard this man's deep booming voice and those words, she smiled in her sleep.

In his dream, YL ran out of the dressing room with the other members of his football team.

"At quarterback today, wearing number 11, Mr. YL Chicken Feathers from Whispering Springs, West Virginia," the voice on the loudspeaker announced. YL saw himself running down the long tunnel of players, the guys slapping his hands along the way. The crowd cheered. People stood along the sidelines and patted him on the back. A football was tucked neatly into the crook of his right arm. His gray-and-maroon uniform was spotless in the autumn sunshine.

Two girls on the sidelines giggled and waved to him. They wore sweatshirts with the messages YL'S STEPSIS-TERS. Miss McPurtle shook pink pom-poms and led the crowd through a rah-rah-rah, sis-boom-bah cheer. Cheerleaders turned somersaults. They cartwheeled onto the field. They blew him kisses. The crowd roared louder and louder with every kiss.

Then, YL ran to the fifty-yard line and stood beside his teammates. The crowd rose to its feet. They whis-tled. They stomped. They chanted, YL—Young Love! YL—Young Love! YL—Young Love!

YL turned. He waved. The football slipped from his grasp. He bent to retrieve it. The players beside him began to laugh. One fell to the ground from laughing so hard.

The whole team pointed at YL.

YL wondered what was wrong. He looked at the football, then looked down, but his uniform had dis-appeared. Instead he was wearing a flouncy hot-pink, crocheted tutu. On his legs, dark purple tights. His feet, neon-green ballet slippers.

"Oh, no!" he shouted. "Oh no, not me!" He pulled at the tutu ruffles. The neon-green ribbons on the dancing slippers tangled into knots. He looked for a place to run, a place to hide.

"YL, YL," a voice beckoned from outside the dream.

YL struggled to listen. Someone shook his shoulders.

"YL! Hey, buddy," Evan said, standing beside the bottom bunk. "YL, wake up. You're having a bad dream."

YL opened his eyes. A cold sweat beaded across his forehead. His heart pounded. "Oh, brother," YL said, wiping his hand over his face.

Evan smiled. "You okay?" he asked. "It's time to get up."

"Yeah, thanks," YL answered.

Evan patted him on the shoulder. "You're welcome, but tell me something, YL, do you always sleep with a football?"

YL sat up. He looked down and was surprised to find his hand neatly cradling a football in the crook of his right arm.

CHAPTER TWENTY-ONE

Cupid's Bingo

"**V**alentine's Day is one of my favorite holidays," Mrs. TenBroeck said on Monday morning, handing out the Cupid's Sweetheart Contest ballots. "Take your time and guess as accurately as you can." She licked her thumb and peeled off another ballot, placing it directly into Stephanie Grissom's outstretched hand. "The person who correctly matches the most baby pictures will win the bag of valentine goodies tied with a red ribbon up there on my desk." A plastic bag bulging with chocolate kisses, bubble gum, red hots, malted balls, and pink nonpareils sat in the middle of the desk. "Ballots are due on my desk by eleven-thirty sharp. We'll have our party later in the afternoon, once I see that you've finished all your work."

Sophie stood beside the bulletin board during TNT and filled in her form. One set of babies in particular gave her a problem. She couldn't decide whether the picture was Carla Clark or Melody Briscoe. Both photographs showed round-faced, blue-eyed, blond-haired little girls in pink dresses.

"So what are you staring at, Sofa?" Melody asked.

"Nothing," Sophie answered.

Melody marked her ballot aloud. "Let's see. Rayna, number fourteen. Harold Pon, number twenty. Emily Willcox, number twenty-one. Sophie," Melody commented, "you've got to be the bowling ball in number three."

"Thanks," Sophie replied.

"And your friend, Stritch, the bitch, is number two." Melody said.

Sophie stopped writing. She didn't see why Melody had to be so mean about Harper.

"Do you want to hear another chapter of the story today, even though it's Valentine's Day?" Mrs. Ten-Broeck asked the class after lunch.

"Will it take away from the party?" Sunday Margolis asked.

"If it does, I don't think we should have it," Charles said.

"Good citizens of Room Seventeen, let's have a little of the democratic process here, shall we? All those in favor of hearing the story?" Mrs. TenBroeck asked.

The vote was 13 to 8. She cleared a spot on the edge of her desk.

"We only have two chapters left," she explained. "We can have one today and then one tomorrow, although we're going to be very busy getting ready for the open house. How many of you have your dioramas ready?" About half the class raised their hands. "Keep working," she said. "I'll be giving out the assignments after the party."

"What assignments?" Sophie asked Bobby Ray.

"The host and hostess assignments," he said, rubbing his hand back and forth over his freshly cut flattop, "for when we have parents visit the room. Mrs. TenBroeck makes us stand at different spots and explain things whenever the parents come in and walk around."

"Oh," Sophie replied, not quite understanding.

Mrs. TenBroeck surveyed the class. "Are we ready?" When she seemed satisfied that everyone had settled down, she began reading.

Chapter Seven: We began walking at first light, Steps Softly and I, my sights set on an inukshuk in the distance. Apoppa and Tiintuk swung from two small bags held around the back of my neck with a thong of leather.

"Ikee, ikee," Steps Softly called before we had gone very far. Cold, cold! How true, I thought to myself with every step, although I felt no fear in feeling the cold. I thought of the song Father sang so often when we traveled. Move through the great world with me. See the moon. Share the stars. Footprints of the sun. Footprints of the moon. Come to the great world. Find its joy.

North. South. East. West. When the time during the winter season revolves around endless night and the sun rises only for a brief moment, directions can quickly become lost. In this half-light of almost night but almost day, I misread a clustering of stones for an inukshuk. Twice, I started off. Twice, I headed in the wrong direction. Before long, I knew deep within my heart that we had lost our way.

I thought of Father. I thought of Mother. Their faces became so clear and shining in my memory. I thought what a good sister Steps Softly was. She held onto my neck gently but carefully and I found that her weight easily became one with mine. But each step I took seemed like twenty in the driving wind and blowing snow. Each climbing motion, each extra effort to set my sites again, only proved more confusing. The lack of food for so many days had diminished my strength, diminished my judgment. I did not know how I could go on. A blowing snow began again, pelting my back and nearly pushing me down at times.

In the end, I marked our spot by stacking stones for an inukshuk of our own, to point me in the right direction when we started once again after the storm had subsided. I found a place for us to sit. I tucked the puppies into a small snow shelter made by the space behind my legs. I carefully removed my mittens and sat upon them. Then I slid Steps Softly around to the front of my jacket, her warm skin comforting mine. She snuggled close to me, resting her head on my chest. I bent over so that I could tuck my caribou jacket around my kamiks. I fashioned for us a small tent of sorts, from my clothing. Then we began the long vigil to wait out the storm. To wait for morning. To hope for the sign of a familiar landmark.

Gently rocking back and forth, I chanted for my baby sister. I chanted for myself. I chanted for my elders. I chanted for the hope of survival. The words became a flowing force coming from a place of need deep within me. I turned my face toward the heavens, carefully weaving the words, then shooting them toward the stars with my voice.

"Once there were two orphans, children of the weather. A daughter to storms, a daughter to snows. Two children, questioning their place in the skies. Drifting among the stars, forming the clusters, whole stories of constellations, whole stories in the stars. The northern lights flashing here. Flashing there. Watch for the signs. Star children running. Star children playing. Their celestial souls inhabiting the night skies. Show us your colors," I sang. "Show us the entrance. Take away our fears. Help us become the many-colored rainbow lights in the night. Children of the northern lights."

The song was gone from me as quickly as it had come. I could hear my own steady heartbeat, Steps Softly's steady breathing. The rhythm of the wind vibrated around my shoulders. Weariness from the day of travel covered me like a heavy blanket. I felt the steady beat of our two hearts, my body cocooning around my sister. Breath upon breath. Life against life. The wind blowing, its constant whistling. I became lost in the sounds, lost in the feelings. Too exhausted, I never noticed as the humming sound of the wind changed to the drone of a rescue plane's engine.

Mrs. TenBroeck quickly put down the book. "All right, my little sled dogs, take out a piece of paper," she suggested, "and let me know what you think's going to happen. Finish the story for me. How do you think *Children of the Northern Lights* is going to end?"

She walked around the room, helping students spell words, pointing out spots where their writing needed a comma, a crossed *t* or a dotted *i*. The class worked until nearly every student had written a five- or six-sentence paragraph.

As she walked around the room collecting the papers, Mrs. TenBroeck said, "Clear off your desks and get ready for the valentines' party."

Once the students had placed their valentines' boxes on the corners of their desks, she began reading a poem from a chart on the wall.

Oh, won't you be my valentine?
My porcupine?
My bodyguard?
Send me a card.
I'll give my all.
My basketball. My brother Paul.
If you'll only say, without delay,
    my valentine you'll be.
Not a bumblebee,
or a chimpanzee.
Give my heart a thrill,

oh, say you will.
Be my ball of twine,
ray of sunshine.
My admiring, inspiring.
My clearly, sincerely.
My super - duper valentine.

Mrs. TenBroeck looked around the room. "I just love Valentine's Day," she said, waving her arms. "Let the celebration begin!" she commanded.

Cheeks puffed out and panting, Carnell Witherspoon won the Bag-of-Wind game by blowing a brown paper bag threaded onto a piece of wire across the entire length of the room with only four breaths.

"Don't pass out on me," Mrs. TenBroeck cautioned, handing Carnell a satin ribbon with a special Class Bag-of-Wind sticker on the top.

Emily Willcox won the Potato Race by walking across the room with a sweet potato balanced on a spoon. Room 17's noise level had increased significantly.

"Shhhhh," Mrs. TenBroeck cautioned, "try and keep it down so I don't get in trouble with Mr. Workel," she explained, handing out the C.U.P.I.D.'s Bingo game cards.

"C three," she called out, reaching into a wire basket for another poker chip with a typed strip of paper

Scotch-taped to it. She watched as the students marked the various letters on the cards with dried lima beans. "P sixteen," she said, looking over her bifocals.

"BINGO! I mean CUPID!" Harold Pon shouted.

Mrs. TenBroeck listened carefully as he read back the letters and numbers he had marked on his card.

"Cutie pie, eleven; Utterly irresistible, twenty-three," Harold said, looking up.

Mrs. TenBroeck nodded. He continued.

"Perspiring palms, three," he read.

"I only have eyes for you, thirty-seven."

"So far, so good," Mrs. TenBroeck said, removing a poker chip from the master grid each time he read a number.

"Devoted, fifty-one," Harold said, looking up.

"CUPID!" Mrs. TenBroeck shouted. She picked up a small bag of chocolate kisses and walked with them to Harold's desk. "Enjoy," she said.

"And now, my little kumquats, we're ready to open our valentine salutations."

She stood beside her desk and began to remove the envelopes marked TEACHER which were inside her hot-pink-and-red-lace-decorated valentine box.

"Thank you," she said, smiling at each student as she acknowledged his or her valentine.

Suddenly, a sorry sound came from the middle of the room.

"Aaaaaaaah!" Melody screamed. "Ooooooh," she cried, dropping the piece of paper in her hand.

"What on earth, Melody?" Mrs. TenBroeck said,

hurrying over to the student's desk. "What's the matter?"

"It's gross, it's gross," Melody repeated. "Oh! Ugh! Oh! Gross!"

Mrs. TenBroeck picked up the valentine. She quickly put on her bifocals. She read aloud, "You may think this is a valentine," then she stopped and followed the arrow's directions, turning over the red-glittered, paper heart, "but it's snot!" That's when Mrs. TenBroeck grimaced. She dropped the red-glittered paper to the floor. "Good heavens! Oh, my word, that's absolutely disgusting."

Bobby Ray stretched out of his seat to see the back side of the valentine Melody had received. He flipped it over with his pencil and shook his head.

"She's been boogered," he hollered. "There are big green, slimy boogers all over the back of Melo's valentine." An audible groan was heard from everyone in the room.

"Who would do such a horrible thing?" Mrs. Ten-Broeck asked, picking up the valentine by a tiny edge. She put on her glasses and carefully looked at the handwriting. She turned to the class and spoke. "You'd better believe me, folks, I'll have a good look at this handwriting. I can't imagine who would do such an evil-minded thing to one of his or her classmates."

She clomped to the front of the room and pulled out a large manila envelope from the bottom drawer of her desk. She opened the flap of the envelope, dropped the

valentine inside, and turned to face the class. "I'm
ashamed of *all* of you!" she nearly shouted. "Imagine
something like this happening in *my* room," she muttered. She stepped out from behind her desk. Bobby
Ray settled back onto his seat, recognizing the oncoming signs of a TenBroeck lecture.

"Now, you tell me," she asked, her face frowning,
"where is your sense of compassion for someone else's
feelings? How could anyone do such a cruel, hurtful
thing?"

"Only one person did it, Mrs. TenBroeck," YL
said, although he realized an instant too late that his
teacher was asking a question that didn't need an answer. "Not every single kid in this class did it," he
mumbled. He sank in his seat as Mrs. TenBroeck
glared at him.

"Not in my eyes," Mrs. TenBroeck replied, pointing
her finger around the room at various students. "When
something like this happens, it's a smeary, black mark
against *every single one* of you."

Sunday Margolis stared at the pencil tray on her
desk. Rayna Abrams picked at a scab on her elbow.
Charles Whiteside flipped the untied shoelaces on his
left sneaker so that one lace landed across the metal
support brace of his desk while the other lace landed
under it. Harper kicked her legs back and forth but kept
her eyes locked onto Mrs. TenBroeck.

"Can you look me squarely in the face, Sunday
Margolis, and tell me that you didn't do a thing like
this?"

"Yes," Sunday said, jumping in her seat. "I mean no, ma'am. I didn't do it."

Mrs. TenBroeck left her desk and patrolled the room, up and down the aisles.

"And you Rayna, did you do such a thing?" Mrs. TenBroeck asked.

Rayna stopped picking at the scab on her arm and looked up. "Nope, it wasn't me, Mrs. TenBroeck. Melo's my friend," Rayna added, smiling like the Cheshire cat.

Mrs. TenBroeck walked over to Charles's desk. "Charles? What do *you* have to say for yourself?"

"Nothing, ma'am," Charles replied, getting very red in the face. "I sure didn't do it."

Mrs. TenBroeck turned and spoke to Harper, who suddenly stopped swinging her legs and crossed them. "And you, Harper? Would you tell me a bald-faced lie about doing such a dreadful thing?"

"Never in a million years, Mrs. TenBroeck," Harper said. "Cross my heart and hope to die," she added, making an X over her heart and holding up her hand in an oath-taking position.

"Hmmmm," Mrs. TenBroeck said, frowning. "So no one's going to own up to this, are they? You realize I'll eventually find out who did this, don't you?"

Sophie trembled.

Mrs. TenBroeck continued: "I have my ways, you know, of finding out who a culprit is." She returned to her desk. "Take out your math books."

"But we've already had math today, Mrs. TenBroeck," Carnell Witherspoon reminded her. He nearly melted like an ice-cream cone on a hot day from Mrs. TenBroeck's stare.

She put on her bifocals. "My dear Mr. Witherspoon. I'm perfectly aware that you've already had math class today. But the way I see it, a little more math couldn't hurt. Now could it?"

Bobby Ray groaned and sank even lower in his chair. Mrs. TenBroeck held the open book in the palm of her hand and flipped through the pages. "Page one hundred and six, everyone. Martin, I want you to come up and write this new assignment on the board, please." He stood up and went to the front of the room. "Write pages one-oh-six, one-oh-seven, and one-oh-eight," she said, turning to him. He began to print. The chalk screeeeeched.

Everyone in the class looked stunned. Three more pages of math! Twenty-five story problems! They took out paper, pencils, and math books. Mrs. TenBroeck was assigning twenty-five story problems.

"Last time it was only ten problems," Bobby Ray whispered to Sophie. "She must be really mad this time."

Mrs. TenBroeck turned around to face the class. "I heard that Bobby Ray McKinnon. That's right, I am upset, but at least make a grammatically correct effort to express yourself. *Dogs* go mad, Bobby Ray McKinnon. *People* get angry. And if I hear any more talking, there will be another five more problems added to what's already there! And," Mrs. TenBroeck emphasized, "you can kiss the last few minutes of the valentine's party good-bye."

The entire class looked up. From that point until the moment the final bell rang, they worked with the resigned diligence of a prison gang digging a mile-long trench.

Thirty seconds before dismissal, Mrs. TenBroeck said, "Tomorrow night is Parents' Night. Don't forget to bring in your dioramas tomorrow morning. I'm going to read off the room assignments. I want you to think about what you'll do at your station. Remember," Mrs. TenBroeck said, taking off her bifocals, "you're the ambassadors for this room."

The students remained motionless while their teacher read from the list she held in her hand.

"YL, Crosby, Aloo, Steve, Charles, Amanda, Stephanie. Art and Music Appreciation."

The seven students all exhaled.

"Carnell, Sophie, Melody. Poetry Center."

Melody glared at Sophie.

"Martin, Rayna, Sunday, Bobby Ray, Suki and Harper. Dioramas."

"Yes, yes!" they squealed.

"Christa, Loren, Emily, Harold, and Carla. Family History Bulletin Board."

The 3:10 bell buzzed.

Mrs. TenBroeck surveyed the room.

"When there isn't a scrap of paper on the floor, you can line up."

Students' feet scuffled around their desks.

"But when do we find out who won the Cupid's Sweetheart Contest?" whined Amanda Washington.

"Oh, my goodness," Mrs. TenBroeck said with true astonishment, "it completely slipped my mind." She checked a stack of papers on her desk.

"I have the results right here," she announced. She put on her glasses and scanned the list. "The winner is," she said, standing up and grabbing onto the bag of candy which had been on the front of her desk, "Harper Lee Stritch."

The class turned to look at Harper who was grinning from ear to ear.

Harper came forward to receive her prize.

"What are you going to do with all this candy?" Mrs. TenBroeck asked as the students lined up to go home. Harper didn't answer. Instead, she ripped a hole into the clear plastic bag with her thumb, walked along the rows of students, and held out the big bag of chocolate kisses, nonpareils, red hots, malted balls, and bubble gum so that everyone in the room could have a piece.

CHAPTER TWENTY-TWO

Parents' Night

Like a nervous butterfly, Mrs. TenBroeck flitted from one spot to another on Tuesday morning. "I always play Vivaldi when there's cleaning to be done," she said, putting on a record. "His music simply radiates energy." She turned and looked around the room. "Everything absolutely spick-and-span," she announced, setting the arm on the record player. "Ah," she said, listening to the music for a few seconds, before giving orders like a drill sergeant.

"Insides, outsides, and undersides," she explained, waving her arm over the desks.

"But no one ever looks on the undersides," Bobby Ray moaned to Sophie.

"All the more reason to do it," Mrs. TenBroeck answered, even hearing him from across the room. "Listen up, ladies and germs," she shouted over the music, "if we can get these chores finished by noon, I'll read you the last chapter in the story for a little R and R."

"What's R and R?" YL asked.

"Mrs. TenBroeck's version is 'rest and recovery,' Crosby explained.

The morning actually flew by faster than YL, Sophie, and Harper ever imagined. Square inch by square inch, the room was swept, dusted, washed, and rearranged. Even the cloakroom looked presentable. Coats, boots, and jackets were hung and paired like in a fire station.

Although the students looked forward to going outside after lunch, Mr. Workel called off recess because of a slow, steady drizzle of rain.

Mrs. TenBroeck assembled the students into a semicircle in the back of the room to finish the story.

"We've had every kind of guess imaginable about how the story will end," she said, pointing to the display of papers thumbtacked to the bulletin board. "Some of you folks used your creative little minds and said that they were rescued by everything from a caravan of woolly mammoths to a set of cocker spaniels that got off course in the Iditarod sled race!"

She put on her bifocals and picked up *Children of the Northern Lights.* "The last chapter," she announced.

As the cold began to encircle me, I felt myself falling into a comforting and endless sleep. This was not an ordinary sleep, but a sleep of many dreams. And in these dreams, the sun was shining. The cold winds had ceased their relentless blowing. Steps Softly opened her eyes and smiled at me. From a distance, I could hear Smoke Lying Close to the Ground, my father, calling my name.

"Stars Beyond Counting," voices echoed from a great distance. "Stars Beyond Counting."

In another dream, I heard Father's voice telling the story of the children who had gone up to the heavens to become stars in the night, swimming through the sky like the many fishes of the seas. The spirits of children, each one sparkling with brilliance, adorned the heavens with brightness.

Had Steps Softly and I become those stars? In my dream, I blinked, trying to look through the darkness to see us as stars. I tried to make my voice ask the question, but I could not make the words. My voice was buried within the center of my chest.

Aiyee! Aiyee! Father! Mother! These words remained trapped inside me, but the thoughts echoed noisily inside my head.

Then suddenly there was the roaring, whirling sound of an enormous bird from the sky. A great weight pushed against my chest. My body shifted from side to side. A rush of warm air caressed my face. Soft, gentle hands. Many hands. Lifting. Carrying. Comforting.

The pilot of the rescue plane had spotted my inuk-shuk. Father's hands were rubbing mine. Not long after that, I heard the sounds of Mother's voice calling my name. Stars Beyond Counting. Stars Beyond Counting.

I awoke to the brightness and whiteness of a medical clinic. The first thing I saw were the worried faces of Father and Mother watching over us. Steps Softly slept by my side, in this quiet place with warming lights. In the following days of recovery, I began to add to the bits and pieces of a story to be told, a story to be told by firelight. This story of mine would be passed down from generation to generation, told at first by my father's gentle voice, the weaving of this tale about his two daughters who very nearly became stars in the heavens. A story told by other Inuit at gatherings, a Netsilik tale about a girl child whose bravery and cunning helped save two lives and the lives of two pups. A true story passed on to even my children's children.

And now by firelight, I, an old woman, continue to tell this story. A story of hunting. A story of survival. A story of sadness and great worry. Yet a story of hope. And with each telling, my story always begins with a poem. A poem spoken to the stars in the heavens. A poem told to the changing darkness of the night sky as it vibrates with the colors of the northern lights.

Arise! Arise to meet the day.
As the first rays of morning's brightness
fill the sky, I search for the threads of light.
Gone is the dark of night.
Morning's welcome daylight shines across my face.
My eyes and heart greet a new dawn
whitening the sky.

And only then can I begin the telling of my story, the story of a time in my life, a time when I was once a brave and fearless Netsilik girl by the name of Stars Beyond Counting.

Tia Mak

"The End," Mrs. TenBroeck said, closing the book. The class sat in silence for a few seconds.

"I'm glad the puppies didn't die," Rayna Abrams said aloud.

"Me, too," Aloo added.

"Did it end the way you imagined?" Mrs. TenBroeck asked.

Some students nodded. Others shook their heads.

Amanda Washington raised her hand. Mrs. TenBroeck pointed to her.

"What book are we going to read next?"

Mrs. TenBroeck made a face as if she were thinking it over very seriously. Then she answered, "In two weeks, we start a unit on United States presidents."

Several students groaned. Mrs. TenBroeck scowled at them.

"Now, it's not that bad. At first I thought about reading a biography of Abraham Lincoln or maybe George Washington. But I recently found a brand-new book in the children's section titled *The Life and Times of Calvin Coolidge*. I thought we might try it."

"Oh, brother," Steve Coffinburger whispered.

"Who's Calvin Coolidge?" Melody asked.

"One of the presidents, stupid," Christa Billetts answered.

*   *   *

By the time the students had finished with gym and art, the end of the day was fast approaching. Mrs. TenBroeck checked one last time on the cleanliness of the room. Desks were realigned. Little scraps of paper were put into the wastebasket that Harold Pon held in front of himself as he walked around the room.

"For all intents and purposes, it appears that Room Seventeen is ready," Mrs. TenBroeck said as the students lined up to go home. "See you back here at six forty-five sharp in your best bib and tucker."

The clock buzzed and everyone scurried out the door.

"Bib and tucker?" Crosby asked. "What's that?"

"Beats me," YL answered.

"Sometimes, Old Tennie comes up with the weirdest stuff," Steve added.

The four boys burst through the double doors and started down the steps.

"Hey, YL," Harold shouted, sliding down the handrail, "we're going to play some football over at the park. Can you come?"

YL smiled. "Sure," he replied. "Sure thing."

The four boys leaped off the last two steps of the Whispering Springs Elementary School and landed on the run, shouting "Aiyee! Aiyee!" as they headed toward the park.

*   *   *

"I'd like to thank you all for coming tonight," Mrs. TenBroeck said to the parents and children standing elbow to elbow in Room 17. Her hands moved when she spoke as though she were directing an orchestra. "The students have displayed their work, and they'll be glad to share their efforts with you. I hope you'll be asking them *plenty* of questions." She walked to the center of the room. "Don't pay any attention to me, whatever you do," she ordered. "I'm only the teacher. The real work in this room is done by the citizens of Room Seventeen," she explained, waving to each group of children standing beside the dioramas, family history bulletin board, poetry center, and art and music appreciation centers.

"They're all yours," Mrs. TenBroeck announced, motioning to the students. "I want you parents to know that I'm extremely proud of every single child in this class." She walked to the art and music center and started a recording of Bach's Sixth *Brandenburg* Concerto.

Sophie stood beside Melody at the poetry center. Several parents put on their glasses to read from the posted sheets of paper. The parents muttered things like "Very nice" and "We never did anything like this in school when I was a kid," eventually moving along to look at the dioramas. Melody twirled a lock of her hair. Carnell shoved his hands in the front pocket of his sweatshirt, and Sophie thought a lot about chewing on the fingernail of the index finger on her left hand, but decided against it.

She watched for her parents, hoping they'd be able to get away from the motel long enough to come over to school. Evan and Lana were visiting Mrs. Cooke's kindergarten room and would eventually come upstairs. Sophie turned to read Steve Coffinburger's cinquain again, when a voice suddenly sent a chill through her spine.

"And what do we have here, Melody?"

A big-bosomed woman in a flowery-printed, tent-like dress towered over Sophie. Melody stepped back.

"For heaven's sake, Melody, stand up straight. Don't slouch, Melody. Pull your shoulders back, Melody. Keep you head nice and tall, Melody. You're not a turtle, Melody," the woman said.

"Yes, Mama," Melody meekly whispered.

"And which poem is yours, Melody?"

Melody pointed to one in the middle of the board.

"And what kind of poem is this, Melody?"

Poor Melody. She looked lost. She fidgeted. Her hand reached for a lock of hair. She twirled it wildly.

"Stop fiddling with your hair, Melody," her mother snapped.

Carnell looked stunned.

Sophie spoke. "These are cinquains, Mrs. Briscoe. They describe the characters from a story we've been reading in class called *Children of the Northern Lights.*"

"And who might you be?" Mrs. Briscoe quizzed.

"Sophie Spagnolo," she answered.

"Oh, I've met your mother," Mrs. Briscoe answered. "Lovely woman. You're that poor family who bought the old Crescent Moon Motel."

"And tell me, young man," Mrs. Briscoe asked, turning her attention to Carnell, "what exactly have you learned from reading one of these foolish children's stories during valuable class time?"

Carnell looked as though someone had sucked the air out of him.

"I think I learned a lot," he began to say. "I learned a lot about the Inuits for starters," he explained. "And I learned how to survive in a blizzard."

Mrs. Briscoe raised her eyebrows and made a face. "Well, isn't that jolly. You'll certainly need that skill here in West Virginia. We have a blizzard once every one hundred years, for heaven's sake!" She stepped closer to the bulletin board. Sophie looked at Melody who had little beads of sweat on her upper lip.

Mrs. Briscoe planted herself at the Poetry Center and read every single cinquain.

"And why doesn't your poem have a sticker on it, Melody?" Mrs. Briscoe asked, tapping Melody's paper with an index finger.

Melody stood silently.

Sophie started to answer, but stopped.

"We'll discuss this later," Mrs. Briscoe told her daughter. "Meet me by the front door, Melody," Mrs. Briscoe said. "I have to visit your sister's room." She swung her large handbag over her shoulder and left the room, sweeping past Mrs. TenBroeck without saying a word.

Melody grew limp. She was as pale as a ghost. "I have to go to the rest room," she said.

Sophie followed. Melody ran down the hallway and pushed open the door to the girls' room with both hands.

She stood by the white basin in the washroom, taking deep breaths. "I'm going to barf," she kept saying.

Sophie tried patting her on the back. "No, you're not," she said.

"Yes, I am, I'm going to barf," Melody repeated.

Sophie pulled two sheets of brown toweling from the dispenser, ran cold water on them, wrung them out, and handed them to Melody. "Here," Sophie said, "I think these will make you feel better."

Melody pressed them against her forehead. Her cheeks were a deep, burning red. "She does this to me every time," Melody said.

Sophie touched Melody's arm. "I'm sorry, Melody," she said. For a brief moment, Melody's eyes met Sophie's and seemed grateful for the consoling words, but within seconds, Melody's mood changed.

"What are you sorry about?" she asked, turning on the cold water tap. Water trickled into the sink. "You ought to be glad she's not *your* mother, Sofa. My mother would have a heyday with a pussycat like you!" Melody splashed cold water on her face.

After a while, the color in Melody's face returned to its natural satiny pink. She walked over toward the door, tossed the brown wads of towel at the wastebasket, but missed. She didn't bother to pick them up. Sophie held open the door.

"So tell me, Sofa," Melody asked as they walked back to Room 17, "what's it like to be Little Miss Encyclopedia about Poetry?"

"You're going to fall right on your noggin if you don't tie your shoes," Evan warned Lana. "Come up here and let me help you." He stood outside the elementary school on the steps.

Lana ignored him. She jumped off the first step. She landed on a lace from her right shoe and sent herself sprawling.

Evan walked down the stairs and was looking at his little sister's skinned knees as YL, Harper, and Sophie came out of the building, heading toward the station wagon.

"Darn," Sophie sighed, "Mom never made it."

"My dad had to work late," YL explained.

"Yeah, and my mom's at basketball finals," Harper said.

"I'm the chauffeur," Evan called to them, helping Lana to her feet. "How about stopping at Mousey's for ice cream?" He held out his open palm and felt the first few drops of rain.

Out of a darkened section of the parking lot, two men suddenly appeared and approached Sophie, Harper, and YL.

"Good evening," one of the men said in a business-like manner, "my name is Joseph Lochinsky and this is my . . ."

The other man stepped out of the shadows. Sophie gasped. The man stared at Harper.

"Rhonda Jean?" he asked, leaning down, holding out his hands toward Harper.

Harper looked at the man. He was squatting, his arms outstretched. Then, without a moment's hesitation, she stepped into his embrace.

"Daddy," she said, melting in his arms.

"Oh, it is you! It is you! My little darlin', I've found you," he repeated.

Sophie, YL, and Mr. Lochinsky stood like statues. Evan and Lana reached the group.

"I knew it was you the minute I saw you," Ronald Eugene Lee said, holding Harper at arm's length. "I took one look at that walk. That black hair of yours. That smile." He encircled her with his arms.

Harper put both her hands on his smooth cheeks.

"And I just knew it was my little girl," he kept saying. "Darlin', I'm here to take you home."

"You will?" Harper asked.

"Absolutely," her father said.

Sophie and YL turned to Evan.

"I'm supposed to give Harper a ride home," he explained.

Mr. Lochinsky spoke to Evan quietly as Harper and her father quickly walked toward their car. "Everything's fine, son, this is her father. This man hired me.

I'm a private investigator. We've looked for her all over the country. We'll make sure she gets home."

But before Evan could think of what to answer, Joseph Lochinsky and Ronald Eugene Lee had helped Harper into a sleek, burgundy car. The last thing Sophie and YL saw of Harper was her small hand waving from the backseat of an automobile speeding away in the drizzling rain.

"Here, kids," the Whispering Springs police officer said to Sophie and YL, "let's scoot your chairs closer to my desk." His warm and friendly voice made being in the chilly office a little easier. He helped them move their folding chairs. "There may be lots of people asking you questions tonight, but I'll tape-record what you say right now so that we have an accurate record."

Mr. Workel cleared his throat from time to time and smiled nervously at YL and Sophie. He placed a small slip of paper on the officer's desk. "We have Harper's fingerprints if that's any help," he explained.

"Thank you," the police officer replied.

Mr. Spagnolo and Evan stepped into the office. Sophie's father spoke to YL. "I talked with your dad, and he's on his way over here." Mr. Spagnolo patted YL on the shoulder.

"I'm awful cold," Sophie said, shivering.

"My fingers feel like ice," YL added.

"Here," the officer replied, leaning down to turn on a space heater. "Let's see if this will warm up the room." He pressed the record button on the tape recorder and began to speak. His voice sounded formal and stiff.

"This tape recording is being initiated by Officer Gilbert Warburton of the Whispering Springs Police Force on Wednesday evening, February fifteenth, at nine-fifty P.M., at the Whispering Springs Police Station. Present are Sophia Spagnolo, age twelve, Evan Spagnolo, age 18, and YL Truax. I forgot to ask you, son. How old are you?"

"Twelve, sir."

"Is YL your full name?"

"Yessir."

"YL Truax, age twelve," Officer Warburton continued. "These two children were the last to see the subject. These preliminary questions concern the disappearance of their friend, Harper Lee Stritch."

Officer Warburton wrote notes on a white pad of lined paper.

"Now, kids, let's start from the beginning. When you walked out of the elementary school building after the open house, two men approached you . . ."

A woman suddenly burst into the office.

"Where is she?" the woman demanded.

Officer Warburton stood up.

"Where's my daughter?" she insisted.

"Are you Caroline Stritch?" Officer Warburton asked, stepping from behind his desk.

She hurried over to YL and Sophie and knelt in front of them. "Where's Harper?"

Sophie and YL looked at each other, afraid to say anything. Evan came over and stood behind them. He put his hands on their shoulders.

Harper's mother looked into YL's and Sophie's faces.

"Harper went with the two men in the car," Evan answered.

"The big man said he was her father," Sophie added. "He told Harper he was taking her home."

The color drained from Caroline Stritch's face. She took in a deep breath and looked away from the children.

"Harper called the man Daddy," Sophie said. "We . . ." she started to say.

"It happened so fast," Mr. Spagnolo offered, looking at Evan, "the kids didn't know what to do."

YL leaned forward. "Is that man really Harper's father? Did he really come all the way out here from Washington to find her?"

"How did you know that?" Harper's mother asked.

"Is Harper's name really Rhonda Jean Lee?" Sophie questioned.

"How did you find *that* out?" Caroline Stritch asked, looking bewildered.

Officer Warburton pulled another chair over by his desk for Harper's mother. He rolled the big swivel chair from behind his desk to the side and sat down.

He spoke directly to Caroline Stritch. "Mrs. Stritch, I need to know if you feel your daughter is in any immediate danger."

She answered slowly. "I hope not. I doubt it."

"Mrs. Stritch, does you daughter need any medications or have any kind of immediate ailment that requires medical attention?"

"No," she answered without looking up, "Harper doesn't have anything like that."

Officer Warburton leaned forward in his seat. "Mrs. Stritch, do you have a court order granting you custody of your daughter while you reside in the state of West Virginia?"

Caroline Stritch opened her mouth to speak but stopped. After a long pause, she admitted, "No, I don't."

Officer Warburton checked the writing on his notepad, then turned to Sophie and YL. "Didn't you kids mention that there was another man at the elementary school with Mr. Lee?"

"Yes sir," Evan answered. "He told us he was a private investigator. He said they'd been looking everywhere for Harper, but I don't remember his name."

Sophie turned to Officer Warburton. "Harper just found out what her real name was when she stayed over at my house last weekend. When she realized her father lived in Tacoma, she tried to call him," Sophie said.

Caroline Stritch looked up.

The police officer watched her for a moment. He pushed the stop button on the tape recorder.

"Mr. Spagnolo, Mr. Workel," the officer said, "I believe that Sophie, Evan, and YL have given me

most of the important information I'm going to need."
Officer Warburton turned to them. "Thanks a lot, kids,
for coming down here," he said, shaking hands with
all three. "You've been a big help."

"What's going to happen to Harper?" Sophie asked
even though she wasn't sure she should.

Officer Warburton looked at Mrs. Stritch, but he
spoke to Sophie. "That's a good question, Sophie,"
he replied. "When there's one child that both parents
want, then courts and the legal system sometimes
have to get involved." He stood up. "The bottom
line is that you kids can go on home. It's late, and I
need to stay here and talk with Mrs. Stritch." He
walked with them toward the door. Officer Warburton shook hands with the two men, then said to Mr.
Spagnolo, "Thank you for coming down." Headlights flashed across the windows of the police station. "That's probably your dad," Officer Warburton
told YL.

Sophie and YL waited by the steps while their fathers and Evan talked.

With the toe of his sneaker, YL kicked at one of the
railing supports. "There's one thing about that guy in
there," YL said.

"What guy?"

"The police officer."

"What about him? I thought he was nice."

YL looked toward the door of the police station. "I
wish he wouldn't call me a kid," YL stated. "I'm not a
kid anymore, and I don't like being called one."

"Yeah, me neither," Sophie said. "I know what you mean."

YL kicked the metal until it vibrated.

"Do you think Harper's okay?" Sophie asked.

"She looked fine to me," YL answered. "I mean, she's found her father and that's what she was trying to do."

"Do you think he took her all the way out to Washington?"

"Probably."

"Yeah, that's what I think," Sophie said. "Do you suppose we'll ever see her again?"

"I don't know. Your guess is as good as mine."

"I hope so," Sophie admitted. "It won't be the same without her. If Harper's really gone, it wouldn't be the same with only the faith and chicken feathers left."

CHAPTER TWENTY-THREE

Four P.S.s

Mrs. TenBroeck opened windows to let the first spring breezes into the classroom two days after the students had returned to school from Easter break. YL erased and rewrote one of the words in the title of his language arts essay: "How I Spent My Spring Vacation." He had titled it "Stepsisters Aren't So Bad, After All." Sophie wasn't making any progress on hers. She chewed on the end of her pencil hoping an idea would come to her. Over the vacation, she'd cleaned her room, gone to the dentist to see about braces, tried to teach Lana to play pool, and watched Evan make goof eyes at Josie Baskim the night she came over to have dinner with the family. When the clock buzzed to go home, Sophie shoved the barely begun essay into her backpack.

"So tell me, you two," Mr. Duke said as they jostled along in old #128 that afternoon, "are you ready for a joke?"

"Sure thing, Mr. Duke," YL said. "I'm always ready for another one of your jokes."

"We're tough. We can take it. It's been a pretty good day, anyway," said Sophie.

"This joke is a new one. Who's going to try it. Sophie? YL?"

Sophie nodded. "I'll be brave." The bus began to slow down before it reached the motel.

"Okay, Sophie, how do you spell mousetrap in three letters?"

She thought for a second.

A car honked behind the bus.

She was tempted to tell Mr. Duke that she didn't know, to give in and ask for the answer without even trying. But YL's quick replies to Mr. Duke's other jokes had left her believing she could think through the answer.

"Come on, Sofe, you can do it," YL urged.

The car's honking didn't help, but Sophie gathered her thoughts together. Mousetraps, mousetraps? she asked herself. A mousetrap was wooden, but wooden was six letters. Trap was four. What else caught mice besides a mousetrap? Suddenly, the answer came to her.

"Cat," she nearly shouted. "Cat," she repeated triumphantly. "A C-A-T, Mr. Duke!"

He grinned from ear to ear, then took a deep breath and removed his hat to smooth his hair. "I guess I know when I've met my match, Sophie," he said with a smile. "You have a nice weekend, you hear."

Mr. Duke pulled the lever to open the bus door. Sophie and YL stopped to pick up the mail before walking up the driveway. They watched Mr. Spagnolo as he worked on the motel sign from a stepladder.

"Hey, troops," he called, "watch this!" He connected two wires. The lights on the motel sign buzzed. Flickered. Flashed, then shone clearly. Brightly. Completely.

Crescent Moon Motel

"Wow! You did it!" YL yelled.

"You got the whole thing this time," Sophie yelled. She and YL stood for a second and gave Mr. Spagnolo the thumbs-up sign.

"Yo, Mom, we're home," Sophie said as they walked through the office, leaving the pile of mail on the reception desk.

Mrs. Spagnolo put on her glasses to sort through the stack.

Sophie and YL were on their way downstairs to the family room when Mrs. Spagnolo called them back to the office.

"Sophie," Mrs. Spagnolo announced, holding two letters in her hand, "these are for you."

Sophie stared at the envelopes. In the upper-left-hand corner of one envelope was Fiddle's address in Magnolia, Delaware. The front of the other envelope only had Sophie's name, address, and Cres Moon Mote. In the left-hand corner was the saying, *Yours*

Till the Computer Chips. The postmark across the stamp showed Tacoma, WA.

"It's from Harper," Sophie told YL. She tore open the envelope, unfolding the single sheet of lime green stationery. She and YL clunked heads as they tried to read the note.

"Good news?" Mrs. Spagnolo asked.

"Amazing," Sophie replied.

"Great news from Harper," YL answered with a grin.

"Do you have any jobs for us right now, Mom?" Sophie asked, unable to stand still.

"No, not right this very second," her mother answered. "Why, what's up?"

"Just give us a half an hour, and we'll be right back," Sophie assured her. She tossed her backpack and Fiddle's letter on one of the chairs in the office, then started out the door with YL.

"Are you going to tell me what's in that letter? Or where you're going?" Mrs. Spagnolo asked.

"Yes, to the first question," Sophie shouted over her shoulder, "and Mrs. TenBroeck's house for the second one. We have super news for her."

"Why, look who's knocking at my door," Mrs. Ten-Broeck said, swinging open the big, white, front door of her house. "What's brought you two over here?"

Sophie held up Harper's letter.

"Sophie just got a letter from Harper," YL explained.

Mrs. TenBroeck motioned the children to come into the living room.

"It smells like cinnamon toast in here," YL remarked.

"I was making a batch of snickerdoodles," their teacher explained.

"This came in today's mail," Sophie said. "It's a letter from Harper, all the way out in Washington. I thought you'd want to hear what she had to say."

"Of course," Mrs. TenBroeck answered. "I've been half sick with worry, wondering what happened to her."

"You won't believe what she wrote, Mrs. Ten-Broeck."

"I'm all ears," their teacher replied.

YL sat balanced on the arm of the couch.

Standing in front of Mrs. TenBroeck's picture window, Sophie cleared her throat and began to read.

> Dear Sofe,
>   Guess where I am? You won't believe it. I'm living in Tacoma. I'm out here with my dad. That's right, MY DAD.

Sophie held the letter so Mrs. TenBroeck could see the capital letters Harper had used. Sophie began reading again.

Would you believe it? I keep pinching myself to make sure it's really happened. I'm spending time with my dad. I'm not sure how long I'll be here, because he and my mom have to get all the legal stuff straightened out about my custody. But I'm pretty sure I'll be back to see you this summer.

Sophie hesitated before she read the next part. She felt like a frog had crept into her throat.

Remember while I'm gone not to let old Melo get your goat. Anytime she needs a good boogering, just let her have it.

Sophie looked up to find Mrs. TenBroeck quietly laughing.

"Did you know Harper was the one?" YL asked.

"Of course I knew," their teacher confirmed.

"But how?" Sophie asked.

"Sophie, honey, teachers know everything," Mrs. TenBroeck explained.

Sophie continued:

> Yours till Niagara Falls,
> Harper, also known as
> Rhonda Jean Lee

Sophie looked up, but went on:

> P.S. #1: Hey, Sofe, you were right.
> My dad's a pretty nice guy.

She looked up again. "Harper likes P.S.s," Sophie explained. As she read the next P.S., she directed her comments toward YL.

> P.S. #2: Ask YL if his initials
> stand for Yugoslavia Latvia. My
> dad and I got out a dictionary
> and that's Dad's guess. And Dad
> says the Seattle Mariners can
> beat the Detroit Tigers any day!

P.S. #3: Tell YL for me that he's not the only one with steprelatives. I found out that I have TWO, can you believe it, T-W-O stepbrothers!

P.S. #4: (I promise this is the last P.S.) My address is: Harper, a.k.a. Rhonda Jean Lee, 1426 Lupine Circle, Tacoma, Washington 98467. Write! I Miss YOU! Tell old Chicken Feathers to write me, too, okay?

Sophie folded the letter and returned it to its envelope. She looked at Mrs. TenBroeck and YL.

"Harper's okay," Sophie told them. "We don't have to wonder about her. It's turned out better than okay."

"Yes," Mrs. TenBroeck said, patting Sophie on the

back. "Yes, you're right, Sophie. I've always believed that given enough time, most things work themselves out, but I certainly earned a new crop of gray hair worrying over Harper. She's got a lot of moxie, though."

Sophie thought for a second, then spoke: "I really do miss her, Mrs. TenBroeck."

"I miss Harper, too," Mrs. TenBroeck admitted. "I'll copy down her address, if you don't mind," she said, taking paper and a pencil from the desk.

"I even miss Harper," YL said, looking a little embarrassed. "I never thought I'd be saying this, but I actually miss a *girl*."

Epilogue

"You drive, and I'll load," YL told Sophie as the two made a laundry run at the motel on a dreary Saturday morning in early June. Sophie hopped into the driver's seat of the Crescent Moon Motel's mobile laundry unit, a small orange, electric golf cart. She cruised along the sidewalk past each motel room doorway while YL dunked piles of dirty sheets and towels into a big mesh basket behind the seats.

"Sophie and YL. Come to the office, please," Mrs. Spagnolo announced over the loudspeaker.

YL slid into the passenger's seat, and Sophie steered the golf cart around the corner of the building and toward the office.

"What's up, Mom?" Sophie asked, pulling open the door as she and YL stepped into the office.

"This box just arrived for you," Mrs. Spagnolo explained, holding a large brown, cardboard carton in her arms and motioning toward the couch. "I think you should sit down. It's from Harper's mother."

Evan, Lana, YL, and Mr. and Mrs. Spagnolo watched as Sophie perched on the edge of the seat. Mr. Spagnolo took a handkerchief from his pocket and began dabbing at his watering eyes.

"Harper's mother is going out to Tacoma to bring Harper home for the summer," Mrs. Spagnolo explained. "She called this morning and asked if we could keep this package for her until she and Harper get back. It seems that what's inside this particular box doesn't travel very well."

"I don't understand," Sophie said, looking puzzled. She noticed that the bottom of the box was warm as her mother set the bulky package on her lap.

Everyone watched, smiling big smiles at Sophie.

"Hurry up," Lana ordered.

Sophie lifted one flap of the box.

"Oh, wow," she exclaimed, her eyes sparkling with excitement.

YL peeked into the box, holding back another flap. "Holy moley," he whispered.

Jupiter's rumbling purr could be heard by everyone in the room. Lana crouched beside Sophie and watched as she lifted up first one, then another, and another black-and-white, splotchy-faced kitten. Jupiter lay on a bed of bath towels and blinked, looking very pleased with herself and her new family.

Sophie handed Evan a tiny kitten. "Jupiter, you really outdid yourself," he commented.

Sophie, Evan, YL, and Lana each cradled a kitten in their arms. One kitten remained with Jupiter, kneading the cat's tummy.

"*Remember, we're only keeping Jupiter and her kittens until Harper gets back in two weeks,*" *Mrs. Spagnolo cautioned.* "*But you know my motto, what's one more when you run a motel?*" *she added with a wink.*

Sophie's kitten used its razorlike claws to climb onto her shoulder. "*Aren't you adorable!*" *she stated. Each kitten was a carbon copy of Jupiter.*

"*Hey, watch it,*" *YL told his kitten as it batted a paw at his nose.*

Sophie turned to her parents and asked, "*Mom? Dad? Can we cook Jupiter and her kittens some macaroni and cheese for lunch?*"

Mr. Spagnolo started to say something but first blew his nose with a big honk. He eventually gave Sophie an answer, but no one in the room was quite sure of his exact response because the words that came out were a jumble of "*as long as I get some, too,*" *and a rather loud* "*ACHOO!*"